P9-CMT-846

THE
LANGUAGE
of
DYING

SARAH PINBOROUGH

THE
LANGUAGE
of
DYING

Jo Fletcher
New York • London

Jo Fletcher Books
An imprint of Quercus
New York • London

© 2009 by Sarah Pinborough
First published in the United States by Quercus in 2016

Any member of educational institutions wishing to photocopy part or all of the work for classroom use or anthology should send inquiries to permissions@quercus.com.

ISBN 978-1-68144-436-9

Library of Congress Control Number: 2016022369

Distributed in the United States and Canada by
Hachette Book Group
1290 Avenue of the Americas
New York, NY 10104

Manufactured in the United States

10 9 8 7 6 5 4 3 2 1

www.quercus.com

For Nick, a good friend, much missed.

"Well, now that we have seen each other," said
the Unicorn,
"If you'll believe in me, I'll believe in you."

Lewis Carroll; *Through the Looking Glass,*
And What Alice Found There

I

There is a language to dying. It creeps like a shadow alongside the passing years and the taste of it hides in the corners of our mouths. It finds us whether we are sick or healthy. It is a secret hushed thing that lives in the whisper of the nurses' skirts as they rustle up and down our stairs. They've taught me to face the language one syllable at a time, slowly creating an unwilling meaning.

Cheyne–Stoking.

Terminal agitation.

New phrases to clog up my mind. I wonder if I'll lose them after. Whether they'll fade and be lost in that place on the tip of my tongue. I don't think so. There are too many association games to play with them.

I'm sitting by the window and from here I can see the small television table at the end of your bed with the video monitor on it. Downstairs, your sleeping image is showing to an empty room—only me here now and I'm here with you. Not that the camera's needed anymore. The *terminal agitations* have stopped. Only terminal trembling remains. And although I know that this means you are closer to the end, I'm glad that part is over. I can spit that phrase out.

Spit, spit, spit. I have become too aware of my own saliva in recent weeks. I can feel it always flooding my tongue, too liquid against my lips. I try to ignore it. Swallow it. I know what it is. Just your disease reaching out and touching me, playing with my head, creating the embryo of a new phobia because it can't quite kill me too.

The clock ticks. I listen to the pauses between your breaths and, although I know that they will get much longer before the everlasting pause takes over, I still find my heart hitching slightly in the gaps. *Cheyne–Stoking.* Ugly as the name is, it can't compete with the meaning. The agitations are ending. The Cheyne–Stoking is beginning. And under all of this is Daddy. At least, I think you're still there. I am exhausted and you are nearly invisible. What a pair we are.

My eyes ache behind their lids as I glance at my watch. Still two hours before the Macmillan nurse arrives for the night shift. For the life of me I can't remember her name. I don't suppose it matters and I don't think I want to remember it. Penny will probably call before the nurse gets here. To see if there's any change. *Any change*. From life to unlife. She knows it's not likely otherwise she'd be here with me, with us, rather than escaping back to *her* life for the evening. She's finding this difficult, but even she can't hide from the fact that life will cling on, regardless of whether it's wanted.

I look at the cup of water and small sponge next to your spit jar by the bed. I think I should dampen your mouth a little, but you seem peaceful and I don't want to disturb you. The disturbances are nearly done for you, I think. I look at the spit jar, the recycled pickle jar once filled with onions and vinegar, and then your body's bitter outpourings and now with blue Listerine mouthwash. Clinically clean. I know that I will never use Listerine again, neither peppermint, nor spearmint, or any other mint.

My anger fights with my grief and threatens to strangle me. I turn away from the sight of you. I can still hear the steady sound of the morphine syringe driver pumping gently under your pillow, keeping you somewhere between this world and me and the nothingness beyond. Or so you would want me to believe; that there is nothing. Your afterlife decision of the past decade. I almost smile, but the tears are too close so I stare out of the window.

It's black outside in the nothing on the other side of the glass, but I still squint and search the fields below. Scanning.

Seeking. Hunting. I haven't looked out of this window for a long time. Not in this way. Not *really* looking. I wonder whether he will come tonight. It's been so long I sometimes wonder if I've ever seen him—*it*—at all. I wonder whether it was just brief bouts of madness. God knows how the wildness of lunacy runs in our blood—no one would be surprised if we all turned out to be fey in some way or another. Maybe the occasional brief bout of madness is all my special gift ever was.

But I still look. Forty next birthday and I'm looking out of the window for something that may be imaginary, that I haven't seen in fifteen years, if ever I saw it at all.

But it's one of those nights, isn't it, Dad? A special, terrible night. A full night. And that's always when it comes.

If it comes at all.

2

Penny is the first of the arrivals. She comes the day after you take to your bed. She comes after my shaky phone call late at night finally convinces her that this is *really* happening; that this really has been happening for six months, no matter how much she tried to smile and laugh and ignore the facts.

When the doorbell goes at just after two p.m.—Penny never could get her shit together before nine or ten—then I know that it's begun. The beginning of the putting-back-together before we fall apart.

I take a deep breath of the air that has been just mine and yours for months. It's been two days since you last smoked a cigarette, but I imagine the lingering tobacco scent filling me up and it gives me the confidence to face the outside. How Penny came to be part of the outside, I'm not quite sure. Maybe we're all on the outside in the end.

The February air is cold as I open the door. She looks wonderful and, even at four years my senior, her skin still glows. She's glowed since we were teenagers, from the inside out, which makes me wonder why she would pump her lips with collagen and make all that natural shine look false. I wonder who she's hiding from.

She steps into the hallway, putting her small suitcase down before reaching up to hug me. "Hello, darling."

"Hello, Pen." I have to lean down a little and, as I breathe in her blend of perfume and expensive foundation, my familiar physical awkwardness returns. She makes me feel too big and clumsy and then that is forgotten and I realize that she's clinging to me too tightly and I squeeze her back until her tears stop. She straightens up and wipes her eyes delicately, but her mascara still smudges slightly. I smile at her from the heart. Sometimes her vanity is endearing.

"Cup of tea? I've got the kettle on."

"Please." She follows me down the creaking corridor. "How's Dad?"

"He's upstairs. I think he's dozing. Do you want to go up? The district nurse will be here in half an hour to see how he's doing. He'll be pleased to see you."

Her eyes flicker upward. "In a bit. I need to get myself together first." She takes off her jacket and hangs it over the back of one of the breakfast bar stools. "God, I can't believe he's gone downhill so fast." Her eyes are still full of water and she shrugs helplessly, pulling the Silk Cut from her Gucci bag. "When I came last month he seemed to be doing so well, didn't he? He was laughing and we were all joking around, weren't we?"

I wonder why she's asking me questions. She doesn't want my answers. I remember that last visit of hers and wonder at our different perspectives. It would have been easy for her to pretend that you were doing well. Just as it was hard for me to see how much effort you were putting into the performance.

I wish I had Penny's capacity for finding the easiness in things. Penny breezes through life regardless of the storm. For me, life has always been the storm. The storm and watching from the window for the thing that could stop it—even if my watching was only with my mind's eye locked on the window of my imagination.

I shrug, put two steaming mugs of tea on the table and take a cigarette from the packet for myself. There is something rebellious in the action and we smile at each other as we embrace the vice that is so meticulously stripping you of your life. We are becoming children again, if just for a while. Sisters. Identical. Opposites. Somewhere in-between.

"I have to warn you. He's lost a lot of weight."

"Yes, he looked so thin last time I came." She pulls on the cigarette and I see small lines tugging at her plumped lips. "Poor Father."

"He must have dropped at least another stone in the past two or three weeks. But you'll see for yourself. I just don't want you to be too shocked." How can I explain that you haven't even been able to keep down the food-replacement drinks? That the six-foot-three oak tree of a man we knew is now bent and hollow, too much skin hanging from your brittle bones. How can I explain that those awful, hacking, choking sessions that used to wake me in the night have now become almost constant? The hangover after any attempt to consume anything thicker than tea. Blessed tea. Kill or cure, it keeps us all going.

Penny puts off seeing you by talking. She talks about everything and nothing, laughing occasionally at strange intervals. I answer when required, but mainly just enjoy her talk. People talk a lot when someone is dying. They talk as if the person is already dead. Maybe it's the first step of the healing process for those inevitably left behind. And maybe you have already started the process by pulling a few steps away from us. The frail used-to-be man in the bed upstairs is not our father. You were so much more than that.

"Have you spoken to the boys yet?" Penny is smoking her third cigarette, normally her total for the day, and the packet of chocolate biscuits we opened is now three-quarters gone. I can feel the gritty remnants in my mouth. I'm very aware of food these days, but I don't remember eating more than the first one.

"No. I thought I'd wait until we know exactly what's going on." She doesn't mean Paul. She means the twins. The twins are always *the boys* even though they're now thirty-five. And if we were all honest with each other then we'd admit to thinking that Simon wouldn't outlast you by more than five years. Not really a boy anymore.

"God, how are they going to deal with this, sweetie? How are they going to cope without Dad?"

"I don't know, Pen. I really don't know. Simon will go one of two ways, but Davey?" I pause, realize how quickly I've become unused to the silence and immediately fill it. "Still, we'll see how he is when we call him." The twins. Davey the paranoid schizophrenic and Simon the junkie, but just *the boys* to us. When I hear other people say they have unusual families, I smile. Our family has so much color that the brightness is damaging.

We talk for a while about all the other relatives that we may have to call: your ex-wife—not our mother, she is long gone in so many ways—the fabulous aunts in London, friends from your time in Australia and Nepal, cousins in Spain and a half-sister in Brighton; all people we claim to love but rarely see. We don't talk about us, though, because neither of us really knows what to say, so we laugh and smoke and eat more biscuits and pretend the years haven't divided us. Eventually, she has to talk about you. Everything else has run dry for now.

"Do you think he's scared?" Penny's voice is small, as if her words will run along the corridor, dance up the stairs and seek out your ears. "He must be, mustn't he? He must have been scared all this time."

"Maybe, Penny. Maybe a little bit. Sometimes." I smile at her and hope it's comforting. "But he's a very unusual man, isn't he, Pen? He says he's not afraid. And I think I believe him. I think I do."

I search inside myself and double-check the words against the facts. Yes, I do believe it. Penny won't though because Penny won't see beyond her own fear. That's why Penny, for all her glow, will never see anything through the window but the fields. Still, I try my best to explain.

"This disease he's got is nasty. I think maybe worse than most other cancers. He can't eat. He can barely drink. But Dad has just got on with it. I can't explain, but if he'd been terrified it would have been so much more awful. It's made it . . ." and looking at my sister and her glow I almost laugh at the irony of my next words, ". . . easier for me."

We are saved from continuing by the doorbell, and I let Barbara, the district nurse, in and introduce her to Penny. Penny's voice becomes more clipped, her accent more refined as she slips into her Gucci persona. If I didn't love her I would tell her that it does her no favors. She is better being just Penny—*Lady Penelope*, as you used to call her way back when.

Barbara's voice is beautiful, though, even when she introduces me to words and phrases that I don't like, that I don't want to learn. She has a soft voice, like honey on a raw throat, the lilt of a West Country accent echoing inside it. And she is kind. Her kindness radiates from her thick-waisted, no-nonsense body as she squeezes my hand.

"I'll just pop up and check he's comfortable. The morphine driver should be taking care of any pain and the night duty team will refill that when they come later." Her ruddy face stretches into a smile and I wonder how a person's mind must work to make them do a job like hers.

"I've still got all his liquid stuff. What should I do with it?" I say. "Can you take it?"

"No, love. You'll have to drop it into a chemist. They can take it from you. I'll get the home carers to call in later too. See if he wants a wash." She rustles up the stairs.

Penny looks at me and I know what she's thinking. What should we do with the morphine when the boys come?

Eventually Barbara comes down and whispers quietly that you are weaker than yesterday, but why don't we poke our heads round the door while you're still awake? There can be no more excuses and I head up the stairs,

Penny following me. It is a little surreal, this turnaround. My big sister—always the one who went first, always the bravest—following me up the stairs, her head down. For the first time in a long time I know that Penny needs me. She needs my strength. She needs me to take the *hard* for her and make it easy.

The corridor seems longer than it has for years. Penny's feet follow mine along the uneven floorboards until we arrive at the door. Penny's nose wrinkles slightly as we step through the doorway and I kick myself. I'd forgotten the smell. There is a scented candle burning on the window ledge and flowers on your desk, but they can't hide the smell of the cancer, a bloated fart hanging in the air. The smell of rotting that escapes with every acidic burp emitted from your poor insides. I look at Penny and squeeze her hand. I wish I hadn't chosen a Christmas candle to burn.

You are propped up on your pillows, your arms out over the duvet and it seems that even since yesterday, even since *I'm not so good today, sweetheart. I've called the doctor. I think I'll go back to bed for a while*, weight has escaped from you, evaporating into the smell that is getting heavier. Your teeth fill your face, your cheeks eat into themselves. Still, you smile a little.

"Hello, darling." Your voice is thinning. I watch you as you hold her hand and I smile sadly as she cries, awkward and uncomfortable. I realize how far along this journey

we've come, me and you. On our own. It's an unintention-
ally secret thing we've done. These last few months can't be
put into words for someone else to take away with them.
And maybe that's why Penny is crying. Because sometimes
easy isn't best.

3

Penny doesn't sit with you long. "He's ever so tired, isn't he?" That's what she says, wiping her tears away. She says it to me as if you aren't even there at all. Perhaps she can't see you underneath your fading body. Her eyes plead with mine. "Maybe we should let him get some rest? We can come back up later." She speaks too cheerfully as she says goodnight to you, her plumped-up lips barely coming near your plumped-up pillows.

She scurries out and I smile at you and you smile wearily back as I stroke your hair and kiss your dry, rotten mouth. "I can see you in there, Dad," I whisper. "Don't you worry. I can always see you." I stay there for a moment, your warmth and mine mixing in the small space between us and when I straighten up your eyes are shut and your breath slow and I wonder if I even said the words at all.

Afterward, Penny and I go downstairs and open a bottle of wine and eat more food, taking trays into the living room. There is toast and biscuits and cheese and ham and pickles and two tubes of Pringles and we scoff them as *Eastenders* plays out its drama in the background; the familiar voice of strangers a comfort, unreality soothing us for a while. We both continue to eat long after our hunger is gone and soon the bottle is nearly empty. My head is buzzing pleasantly, the world shimmering at the edges. I'm not a good drinker, not like Penny. But I think she's a little drunk too. Her feet are up on the coffee table next to the surviving crumbs of our feast and her head lolls sideways against the brown leather.

"I would have had him come and stay with me; you know that, don't you, sweetheart? But with James being so little and the au pair living in, it would have been . . ." Her petite shoulders shrug as if the rest of the sentence is so self-explanatory she needn't waste her breath on the words. I'm tempted to say, *It would have been what, Penny? Too hard?* but I swallow my sharp tongue along with my sharp white wine, letting them both fizz angrily inside. I could say those words. And they would be true. It would have been too hard for Penny. And there's the dry fact and no anger will change it and that's why I stay quiet and keep my understanding silent. Different horses for different courses. You were always going to come here. Back home with the middle child. The pivot, the hinge between the *normal* of Paul and Penny and the strange, mad world of the boys; sometimes tilting this way and sometimes that. In both camps and yet neither.

Penny is still talking and making excuses that aren't needed, but she needs to hear them out loud in order to believe. She talks and I find myself drifting. I've always drifted. Sometimes there are just too many words filling up the space and not enough emptiness left for thinking. I keep a little emptiness inside for when I need it. *She's off again.* That's what you used to say, way back when. *Hey, Lady Penelope. Nudge your sister, she's off again.* And then you would laugh. *In a world of her own, that one.*

Time is surreal. I can hear that laugh as if it were yesterday and in the same instant I can see the years ahead in which I will never hear it again. I squeeze my eyes shut let the drifting take over.

They think I'm a dreamer, Paul and Penny. They think I don't live in the real world, and maybe I don't. Maybe I've avoided that, because if I cement myself too firmly in the *here*, then the thing outside the window, the thing in the field, will no longer exist. And if I were to allow that then it would be lost to me for good. I know this as surely as I know you are dying and that *you* are nearly lost to me for good. Nothing I can do will change that.

But, despite my empty thinking space, despite Penny and Paul's sideways glances and rolled eyes over the years, it was only me who understood the seriousness of things a year back when your swallowing problems began. It was only me whose insides screeched with the knowledge of your life's unraveling. It was only me who asked the questions and wanted to hear the answers. I can see the irony, even if they can't. My *own world* is more real than theirs, even if I am lost in it. I don't hide behind my cars and my clothes and my plumped-up lips.

Yes, you were always going to pack up your small flat and come back home. Because I think maybe you are a drifter too. We understand each other.

The silence breaks my thoughts and I realize that Penny has stopped talking and is looking at me, waiting for an answer. I have no idea what she has said and I know that she knows I've been gone *in a world of my own*, so I just smile and she smiles back. She runs one hand over my head gently, as if the four years between us are still a huge divide and she is still my big sister rather than a woman I once knew. But still, I am happy that she's here. It's a big warm rush coming out of me, like waters breaking and I look at her and think how I have envied her and hated her and avoided her over the years and yet here we are. Sisters again.

But then love clings on, doesn't it, Dad? Even when by rights it has no place left to be, love is hard to kill. Like life. And sometimes, like life, it takes you completely by surprise.

There are enough bedrooms, but Penny and I choose to share one bed, enjoying this closeness that both of us are too afraid to mention in case it crumbles, its solidity unsure. The duvet is pulled up under our chins even though the room is too hot. The heating throbs through the pipes, gurgling like the slowing blood in your veins, both determined to keep you warm and alive for as long as possible. It won't be long until my skin starts to itch with sweat, but I don't mind. We are all cold in the end.

Penny is talking and I am determined not to drift, but to listen, to feel the glow that escapes with her words as she recalls incidents from so long ago. Lying there, we remember and laugh and it feels so good, mainly because I know that it will never be the same again. It is bittersweet. As you let go, so shall we. Buried in the scent of fresh sheets and the warmth of my sister, I store each second safely away so that I can savor this time in the years to come.

Still, tonight we talk about the old days and pretend they were as funny then as they are now. The times when you were really drinking hard, after Mum had gone and you had remarried and we were living through the "Shetland experience" as Davey refers to it.

Yes, you were—*are,* not were yet—a drifter. Only a drifter would think it was a good idea to take five children and your new wife to the middle of nowhere and that it would pull you all together instead of ripping you apart. But then, if you pour vodka on your cornflakes every morning for four or five years, you're going to have a lot of crazy ideas. A drinking drifter, that was you, our dad, way back when.

I don't even know what Penny is trying to say, but we are laughing so hard I think I may wet myself. And then I spoil it.

"I wonder if Dad can hear us laughing." The words come out with a giggle, but the sound is wrong. We quiet down after that, the atmosphere broken. I feel like we are in a bubble in the bed, a moment of *alltime*, not just then or now or in the time when you are no more, but all of it together, inseparable. For a while we say nothing, just listen to each other's breathing and the rustle of eyelashes betraying wide-awake eyes.

It's Penny who cracks the silence with her soft voice, but this time we don't laugh. We talk about the night Mum left us. Not when she died, like you will soon, but when she just upped and left.

Penny sniffs a little, still recovering from all the belly laughing and I fight the urge to squeeze her tight. There, in the dark, the years have evaporated and she is just my big sister lying next to me, all natural and glowing and undamaged by life.

"What happened to you that night?" I can almost hear her brow furrowing in the sound of her voice. She'll regret that, my empty thinking space says. More lines, more injections.

"What do you mean?" My eyes adjust to the dark and I make patterns out of the shadows and shapes of the plastered ceiling. I think it's human nature, isn't it? To look for patterns or meaning in things? That's what Penny is doing now.

"You were almost hysterical. We found you out in the field in the middle of the night. You must remember." She pauses, maybe doing a little drifting of her own, back to that night. "I woke up and you weren't in bed. What made you go outside? You never said."

"I was ten, Penny." I state that as if it is enough, and maybe for Penny it is.

"Were you looking for Mum? Did you think she'd change her mind and come back for us?" Penny has found a pattern, a meaning that she can understand, and she keeps hold of it.

"Probably. I don't remember much about it."

"You are a funny one." Her voice is more settled. "Took hours to calm you down. You kept getting out of bed and going to the window."

She sighs and we drift into our own worlds. Bubbles within bubbles. She has accepted my lie because it fits in easily, but it's still a lie. I remember everything from the night our mother left. How could I forget? It was the first time I saw it. Lying here in the dark, in this moment of *alltime*, I let the memory run into my skin.

* * *

There are a lot of jazz records played in our house, it is the one tenuous bond Mum and you share beyond alcohol and the call of wild blood; a love of music that blares and dances and laughs like you do. Like you do in the good times. There's a lot of jazz and a lot of rows and a lot of broken glass hidden amongst the books and the university papers and the vodka and wine bottles that make up your lives.

We are living in Surrey, in the house you inherited from your parents and which I will eventually buy from you. It's large and untidy in a pleasantly middle-class way, but isn't quite big enough for our ever-growing family and the piano and the various rabbits and hamsters we collect. We are a dysfunctional clutter of children who play within its walls when school is done. Paul, Penny, and gradually I, begin to suspect that although we speak as politely as the other children in our suburban grammar school, our home lives may not be quite as ordered as theirs. We don't invite friends round and we decline invitations to tea. We do these things without consultation, each sibling owning their individual moment of revelation. My moment comes when you collect me from school one day. I am six, it is the seventies and things are "looser," but even then all the other fathers either have their shirts tucked all the way in or hanging all the way out, their clothing delineating their political sway. Your shirt, though, is somewhere in-between, ignoring your politics. A bit of it is crumpled into the waistband of your trousers, but most of the back remains untucked like the boys at the big school wear them. I know that it's wrong in a not-quite-right way and then I realize that is the same for everything in our family. Not-quite-right, not-quite-wrong. Too many cracks mar the surface.

I don't look at the children and parents casting sly glances in our direction. *Is he drunk?* I can feel the hum of their whispers with every footfall. At least you are there to collect me while Mum sways to jazz in the garden and doesn't work on her university thesis. You don't leave us. You will never leave us.

Our mother loves babies and even as children we know this. She loves the touch and the smell of them. She loves their wriggling need and the way the crying stops when she wraps them to her thin chest. Of course we stop crying. Two parts breast-milk, one part raw spirit is what flows out of her and into us. She delights in babies, our mother, but not in motherhood. She has no interest in that. Children with *minds of their own* and a will separate to hers exhaust her. When we get to the foot-stamping age her love affair tires and it becomes time for another, fresher, smaller child to satisfy the aching place inside her only an infant can reach. Paul is the first to be discarded and then Penny, and then me.

By the time the boys come along things are falling apart for our parents and not even the joy of two temporary slaves to her breast can keep our mother with us. They disappoint her by quickly growing chubby limbs that support themselves. I think maybe they disappoint her more than we did. The boys rely on each other for play and comfort in that special way twins have that excludes all others. By the time they are coming up to five she starts to dislocate. She is still there, but she stares emptily at us as if wondering how on earth we all came to be. And it is you that makes the tea as best as you can and puts us all to bed.

Too often, too late at night, jazz is played too loudly to drown out slurring arguments that spark from nothing on the dry, dead twigs of our parents' marriage. It becomes habit. Our middle-class bedtime lullaby.

Jazz is playing the night she finally leaves, when I am just two weeks into ten years old.

I am tucked up in my small bed, the covers almost all the way over my head. My bedside lamp is still switched on even though it must be gone ten. I think that Penny will turn it off, if she comes back to our room. We know that our parents will not be checking on us so Penny crept over to Paul's room as soon as the volume was turned up; Miles Davis cheerfully trying to distract from the sounds of our parents' war of self-loathing and mutual frustration. Two alcoholics staring at each other and not liking what they see, only a reflection of themselves, nothing better. Nothing worth loving.

Penny has started going into Paul's room a lot and I know that they think I am too childish to share their talk and their games. Not as much of a baby as the boys but still not old enough to join in. There is just over a year between them and they are becoming their own branch on our family tree. They share knowing glances and giggling fits across the tea table. I feel lonely in my middle perspective, looking down at two who don't need me and up at two who are too adult for me.

Tonight the music can't drown out the rage and our mother shrieks her tantrum, all the words becoming one animal howl through the plaster of the ceiling. My heart is beating fast in my chest, discordant with the record and with the row. There are hot, wet tears on my cheeks, but I don't sob. I pull the covers further up over my head and wish I could remember a song to sing myself. Something that isn't jazz, that isn't wild, but my head is empty. After a while of listening to the pounding thump of blood pushing round my body, feeling my own hot breath beneath the blanket that threatens to choke me, I realize that the sounds from below have stopped. Only the jazz is playing cheerfully on, uncaring about its silenced accompaniment.

I push my clammy face out into the light and listen. There is nothing below the music. The carpet is rough beneath my feet as I go carefully out into the hallway. Paul and Penny are sitting silently on the top stair. They look at me with their matching wide brown eyes.

"I think Mum's gone," Paul says. He is nearly sixteen and his unruly hair goes this way and that, like his voice that hasn't quite broken. Paul isn't broken yet either. Not yet damaged goods. Or maybe just a little.

Penny is holding his hand so tight that even in the gloom I can see where the blood is being squeezed aside. Her eyes are filling up, but to me she still looks beautiful.

"I don't think she's coming back. She didn't even say goodbye. She didn't look up once."

Paul hugs her and I say nothing, but my hands grip the sides of my polyester nightie and I pretend I am holding someone else and then, as my heart picks up the pace and sobs convulse my chest, you come up the stairs and sweep me off my feet, your warm tobacco smell enveloping me.

You take us into the boys' room and talk. You talk a lot and none of it really means anything to me. You talk about guilt and blame and love and other things in the gray area we only understand in a black-or-white way, but we all know in our hearts that it's our fault for not staying little for long enough.

Listening to you and seeing you try to be sober and try to give enough love for two and try to understand where it all went wrong, I wonder if you are too stuck in the gray to see the truth of our mother. Babies are wonderful, children tie you down. They make you old. And she has far too many of them. You blame yourself of course. And you

will do for years to come. I think for all the years before
you stop drinking.

Penny asks questions and cries and for a while Paul
shouts at you and then the twins start to cry and we all sit
silently. I yawn, suddenly wanting to be back in my bed
and then everyone's mouths stretch wide including yours,
me the leader for once, and although there is emptiness
inside all of us, the calm is good. The calm is very good.
We go to bed, shuffling to our own corners of the house.
The light goes off.

I can hear the clock ticking on the top of our shared
chest of drawers. I listen to it until it fills my head and
makes my ears hurt. I don't sleep. My eyes are so heavy,
but my heart is pounding and my head feels too hot. From
Penny's bed a few feet away, the sound of tears, of *tears*
in her heart, has stopped and her hitching breath is now
steady and slow. She doesn't even twitch, so lost is she in
sleep. Her body has shut down to close out the hard and
let her start to recover. Gazing upward in the dark I envy
her. My body is storing the storm and I wish I could just let
it out. My feet itch and, quietly pushing back the covers, I
get out of bed, go to the window and kneel on the carpet.
I slip my head under the curtains, goosebumps instantly
appearing on my skin as the temperature drops a couple of
degrees, night air sneaking in through the tiny gaps around
the sash window. Until Penny grew up and found Paul,
we often snuck out of bed and came and rested our heads

on this window ledge, giggling and making up stories of princesses and witches and happy endings.

Now, sitting on numbing ankles, the curtain feels like a shroud around my dying childhood and even in the chill my face gets hotter and hotter, burning me from the inside out. I wish I could cry; I wish Penny would come back from being a teenager and I wish Mum would come home and put everything back to not-quite-right. Something is building, bubbling in my stomach, flaring into white heat and I don't know if it will explode out of me or whether it will meet with the dark spots at the edge of my vision and make me pass out. I want it to come out in words that I don't have. I want it to make sense. To be not-just-mine. And then, as I am about to combust, it appears in the night. Out of nowhere.

There is a road between the end of our garden and the fields beyond. People drive too fast down it, eager to get to the next town—to other people and away from the quiet. At one a.m. though, it is silent and empty under the white light of the streetlamps, safe for hedgehogs and country mice to cross.

The creature in the middle of the road staring up at me isn't one of these scurrying through the night. It stops my breath racing from my lungs as I stare in wonder. It wasn't there a second before. There was nothing there but tarmac. And now here it is. Inside, the white fire I can't control cools slightly. Below, on the cold road, its red eyes glow angrily and through the glass I can see hot steam charge from its flared nostrils as it paws the ground. I think perhaps it is blacker than the night, its mane shining as it is tossed this way and that. I am not sure whether it is beautiful or ugly, but I know that it's wonderful. And I know that it's waiting for me. One of my hands rises to the cold glass, as if by touching that I can reach the beast below. The lonely emptiness inside me fills up with something warm and thick. This creature and I belong together. I know it and so does he.

Its body is large, like a horse but more solid—without the elegance but with twice the power. I can see thick sinews bunch along its long neck as it raises its head again, glaring at me. A black horn grows twisted from between its eyes, a thick, deformed, calloused thing, a tree root erupting from the earthy ground of its forehead, the matt texture oppositional to the sweaty shine on its dark hide. I stare at it and our souls meet. It is power and anger and beauty and nature rolled into something other-worldly, waging a war with the night on its four thick hooves.

I can't breathe for a second and then the black beast rises up on its rear legs, frustrated at my inaction. It is perfection to me, not like the white, insipid animal of legends with which it shares it horn—that creature does not exist. This one exists more plainly than I do. It is gnarled and dark and full of passion and I know that if I could bury my head in that mane it would smell of the earth and sweat and blood.

It glares at me and I know that below it is whinnying, a deep throaty growl of a sound. A terrifying sound. I smile. I can't help it. This instant I am full of joy, pure and bright.

I bite my cheek and stare in disbelief as the furious creature turns, its eagerness to travel through the night too great. Without looking back it jumps heavily over the fence, becoming invisible against the night. It is gone, its patience worn thin. It has no more time for me.

The light inside me goes out leaving only the white heat of pain.

The heat burns my face and burns my brain as I push away from the floor, my legs bursting with energy as I run in panic into the night. I think a whine escapes me, high pitched. I will not be left behind. I will not.

I feel nothing after that. I can barely think; the world is a mess as I drift in the worst way. I know that the tarmac hurts my feet and I know the mud of the field is thick and cold and sucks me down. I see the last glint of bright eyes in the night before there is only the dark and my hot tears. I know I fall. I think I call out. I think I am still screaming, "Come back! Come back! Don't leave me behind!" when you, Penny and Paul find me on my filthy knees, sobbing in the darkness.

I remember everything from the night our mother left us. So many years ago, and yet still with me. Bubbles within bubbles. I quietly raise myself up on one elbow and look at Penny. She is sleeping, her hands tucked under her cheek and her knees pulled up into her chest. I smile and stroke her hair before quietly pushing back the covers, happy to be out of the heat. My eyes are wide open and they burn when I blink. My heart beats too fast to sleep and I want to shake off the feeling of *alltime*.

Leaving the light off I pad down the long, dark corridor and sit with you for a while, even though you are sleeping too. I don't speak; I just watch you. I resist the temptation to go down on my knees and slip my head under the curtain. I only allow myself one quick glance out. The road is empty. There is nothing in the field. And I wonder again if there ever really was.

4

By nine a.m. the breakfast bar is covered with the remains of our huge fried breakfasts and the scent of hot grease clings to our hair. I have pulled on some jeans and a T-shirt, but Penny has managed to apply full makeup in the same amount of time. I wonder how she does it. While we wait for the doctor I ring the library and tell them I won't be in for a few days. My father is dying. The words feel odd in that order and they make the woman on the other end—I think it's Shirley, but I'm not sure—close down.

Hearing the language does that to people. There are no questions. They don't want to hear about it. They don't like the little bit of the language they already know; they don't

want to add to it. And I can hear all of this in the closed
tone of Shirley's voice. I hang up and wonder if I ever told
them that you were sick or just that you were coming to
live with me. I don't remember. I don't care. The world
outside the house no longer exists. Not for a little while
anyway.

We drink tea and are just finishing the rest of the chocolate biscuits when the doctor arrives. He is a large, middle-
aged man. A fat man who speaks very little and appears
preoccupied when he does utter a few words. I offer to
show him where you are, but he waves me away and takes
his black bag upstairs, leaving us clinging to our cups of tea.
We go back to the warm comfort of the kitchen, matching his heavy footfalls as he heads toward your room. We
eat more biscuits until he comes back downstairs. The
chocolate makes me feel sick as it hits the eggs and bacon
and toast already in my stomach, but eating is better than
talking. We think we know the answers anyway. I can see
them in Penny's scared, kohl-lined eyes. We think we know
exactly what the doctor is going to say. We think your time
is nearly up. In our hearts we know that you will be dead
by tomorrow. After all, you look so ill and haven't drunk
anything for twenty-four hours. Open and shut case.

We are very surprised then when the doctor's closed
face remains calm and detached. Penny is rambling on
about the folder the nurses left last night, and where
should we keep it, and how often should they write in it

and then I cut her off. "He's dying, isn't he? How soon will it be? Should we get the rest of the family?"

The doctor shakes his head vaguely, unaware of the panic in my voice. Or maybe he is just immune to it with this job of his. He shrugs.

"He is very sick. I think he has a week. Not much more than that at any rate. Maybe a day or so less."

I stare at him as if I've been slapped in the face. Beside me, Penny too is silent.

"But he can't eat and he hasn't drunk anything for at least a day," she says.

The doctor shrugs. "Yes, he's very dehydrated. Try and sponge his mouth. Maybe with juice as well as water. Pineapple juice is a natural cleanser and might give him some energy. The acids and enzymes in it work well in the mouth." Penny nods and quickly scribbles down *pineapple juice* on a piece of paper dragged from her handbag. She has always liked lists. They help her feel in control.

"A week? Are you sure?"

The doctor looks back at me and nods. "The body fights, you know?"

After a moment I nod back as if I understand and perhaps I think I do. In fact, I know nothing. I am so naïve. Penny has started talking again and she talks the quiet fat man all the way to the door. Standing in the kitchen, I wonder at death. You look so sick. You've given up. You haven't drunk anything. I think this should surely be enough to make death take over. I am wrong of course. You have so much more dying to do yet. You have to become so much less before you go. The doctor is, in fact, spot on. One week. Maybe a little less. The body fights, you know?

Now I do.

When the doctor is gone I go up to check on you, but you don't seem to know I'm there. Or maybe you're just ignoring me. I wouldn't put it past you. I say as much and laugh as I leave the room, as if everything were normal. Or at least not-quite-right normal.

By the time I get back to the kitchen, to the warm heart of our microcosm world, I am crying. Penny looks at me and then she is crying too. We cry at each other for a while and then we make more tea, light cigarettes and make lists. I am sure Penny's list has a function, is organized, but I look down and see mine is just a jumble of words on a small sheet of paper. I have written *morphine/pineapple juice* as if creating a new cocktail. And maybe I have. Maybe it's a Dad special. Then the words are blurred as my eyes and my nose run free.

We eventually talk about the boys coming. I can feel the tension rising before we've even started the calls. Penny's list of people we need to contact is getting longer, but I think maybe the best way to start is by looking through your little address book. I fetch it from its place by the phone and flick through the yellowed pages, looking at the numbers and words laid down in your neat, scratchy hand. My heart clenches.

You won't be writing again.

Not ever.

The finality of the thought is cold and makes me shake. I am so tired. It's been a long few months and, even though time has folded from the first diagnosis to now, my body and soul know that I have lived through every painful second of it. They sing it to me through aching limbs and a torn heart. I am not very strong. I never have been. I hand the book to Penny.

"All Dad's numbers are in there." She looks at it as if it's something sacred and not a ninety-nine pence stocking-filler address book from WHSmith. "If you ring Paul, then he can ring the boys. They all need to come and say their goodbyes." The words don't feel adequate as I say them. "I'll go to Tesco's and get some more food in. I'll call Mary and some of the others when I get back." I start gathering my purse and bag together. I still have my jogging bottoms on and I haven't showered, but I don't care. The supermarket will have to put up with it.

Penny pulls on her cigarette. "Oh God, what am I going to say? What am I going to say to Paul?"

I look at her. I know where this is heading. "Just tell him what the doctor said. Tell him Dad is dying and he needs to come now."

Her perfect eyes are pleading with me. "Maybe you should call him. You're better at this kind of thing than me."

I grit my teeth. *What kind of thing, Penny?* I want to scream. *Clearing up the crap?* For a minute I look past the makeup and expensive perfume and see only the worst parts of my sister. Selfish. Spoiled. Damaged by her glow. I feel bitter and I can't stop it. Penny has always had Paul—the two of them are thick as thieves—and the twins have each other. I have you and now you are concentrating on leaving me.

"You do it, Penny," I say, and then she stays quiet.

There are more people in Tesco than I expect on a working day and I lose myself in them as I drift up and down the aisles, filling my trolley with bacon and eggs and pineapple juice. I select a box of field mushrooms and then stare into the aisle. The lights overhead are too bright. A tired mother adds the large bag of King Edwards she'd obviously forgotten into her already overfull trolley, while the little boy in the child seat kicks at his metal confinement, squealing, "*I want, I want . . .*"

I can't make out what it is he wants, but I think maybe his mother will give in and get it for him just to find a moment's peace. She is pretty but looks exhausted and I wonder if I've caught her at a bad moment or whether she lies in bed at night and wonders how her life came to this.

Behind them an old man carefully pulls a plastic bag from the holder and selects three or four new potatoes. Just enough for one. He adds them to his sparsely filled basket and shuffles slowly toward the tomatoes. I can't tell if the shuffle is brought on by age or by sheer soul-weariness. Behind me I can still hear the cry of "*I want.*" It seems that age is all around, brought to nothing under the glare of the too-white light and inane music. My throat tightens in a way it hasn't for a long time and my ears buzz. Somewhere underneath my heartbeat and dry mouth I wonder if I might abandon the trolley and run back out into the cold air of the car park. But then the moment passes.

I relax my grip on the trolley and rub my fingers. They are cold. My heart steadies and I continue my shopping, but I focus hard on the shelves rather than the people. When the old man passes me again I squeeze my eyes shut so tight that I think I can hear the pummeling of black hooves somewhere in the distance, but the panic doesn't grip me again and I open my eyes and sigh out a long, shaky breath. I add the ketchup I'm staring at to my trolley.

By the time I get home I feel a little more stable. I am nearly forty, I remind myself. I can cope. The house is quiet. I go into the kitchen with the first run of bags and Penny is crying.

"I've rung Paul," she says. "He's going to ring the boys. I told him he's the eldest brother, it's his job. You're doing enough." She doesn't look up. She is looking at sheets of paper pulled from an open folder. I recognize the folder. It is red cardboard, like so many of his others, but for the words *funeral arrangements* scratched on the flap in black pen. Penny is staring at the receipt and the paperwork.

"Did Dad do this, or you?"

My shoulders ache as I put the bags down. "Dad. He did it while I was at work. Hang on." I go back outside and fetch the last of the bags, slamming the boot. Pen doesn't come out to help. She won't have thought about it. Air to my earth. When I go back into the kitchen she's unpacking the first lot, though, tidying the fridge as she goes. She lines up the margarine and the eggs so that they are at perfect angles with one another on different rows.

I've watched Penny over the years and I think maybe her need to clean and tidy is a little on the compulsive side. I think she will forever seek the order she's never found in her life, despite her glorious adventures and her romances and her children. She cleans, she scrubs and she tidies. Her house is spotless when I visit and I know that it is always spotless regardless of visitors, and I wonder sometimes what it really means, this need to be clean. To be *seen* to be clean. Watching her rearrange the fridge so officiously I wonder if I really know her under the glow at all.

I throw the mushrooms into the vegetable rack not really caring where they land. This is my order.

"He had about three funeral companies round one afternoon and basically figured out which one did the best deal. He's paid for it already. The car and flowers and everything." My tone is conversational and I feel as if we're talking about you booking a holiday. Maybe it's better that way. "He's having a wicker coffin. He wanted cardboard but it was more expensive. Figure that one out."

I don't tell her about the evening we spent trawling the Internet, examining the biodegradability of various coffins. I wouldn't be able to say it and she wouldn't get it. Penny laughs from behind the fridge door. "Only Father . . ." It warms me to hear her laugh. It's a good sound.

"Yep," I say. "Only our mad dad."

She laughs some more at this and as I join in I wonder where laughter fits into the language.

When the shopping is put away, Penny goes to have a bath. I wonder why she bothered putting on all that makeup and then I remember she's already showered once this morning. I think about the bath and put the immersion heater on so there will be enough hot water for me later. Baths are not about washing. They're about soaking. Floating. Drifting privately in the warmth. Maybe that's what Penny wants. Some private time. I don't mind. I understand private time and it's good to have the kitchen to myself again. I look outside. It's raining. I open up the window and put my face into it, stretching my neck. The fresh, dewy smell fills me up and the water hits my skin in tiny slaps. For a moment the sensation is exhilarating, but then the cold and damp are too real and I shrink back into the shelter of our home. I settle for watching the water streaming against the glass and trees, the drops erratically chasing each other before becoming one on the windowsill or the ground. I could watch for hours, mesmerized by the everything and nothing of nature.

It was raining like this on that Sunday morning when we went to see the crematorium. Another bubble of time.

The windscreen wipers scratch across the glass in a steady rhythm, smearing the water. You sit beside me. You tell me I need to get *new bloody wipers* before they ruin the screen. I bite my tongue to stop myself saying that all of this is too bizarre, because you already know it is—just as I know I need to get new bloody wipers.

We are silent as I pull off the clinical grid road and follow the sign down a sweeping drive. Even though it's raining and the grounds look beautiful, I can't help but think of Dachau or some other death camp. I look to the sky, half expecting to see a plume of black smoke rising and pressing against the gray clouds. It isn't there, of course, but I see it through the window of my mind, far too clearly. I see a lot of things I don't like through that window.

"Are you sure you want to do this?" I ask you, although the question screams inward, at me. Only our mad dad, I think. Only our mad dad would ask me to do this and think that it's fine. You smile at me and nod, and I see how tired you are, just the act of leaving the house draining more hours and minutes away. I smile back. You put the small plastic sputum tub into your pocket. You carry it with you everywhere now, just like your tobacco and lighter. The yin to the smoke's yang. But then all that spit has to go somewhere and it can't go down, so it has to come out. Surreptitiously, though, and when no one is looking, because spit is rude, spit is wrong and you are always such a polite man. It doesn't make me heave anymore when I see it. Not like it used to.

I get out of the car and zip my jacket up so that it's nearly touching my nose. Sometimes, at home, when you're using the jar, I concentrate hard on the TV so I don't have to catch sight of the tobacco-brown slime that escapes from you as you cough and choke it out. I don't let you see my discomfort. I don't want you to know that I've started to hate the feeling of my own wet spit flooding against my tongue. I'll get over it. You won't. Time will heal me. Time will take you from me.

We don't speak as we hunt out the office, our feet crunching on the gravel, disturbing the silence. The rain patters lifelessly to the ground. It's thinned since we left the house; only drizzling now. Through the window of my mind I see an aging, fat God sitting above us in stained underpants, hacking and choking as he sends his saliva down in rain. It's a comical image, farcical. My mind does that to me sometimes.

You are striding ahead and I run to catch up. There is no breeze or wind and it should be cold, but it isn't. There is a nothingness to the weather, and although I normally like the fresh chill of water on my skin I don't want it today. Too much water. *Too much water under the bridge.* The phrase makes no sense, but I think it anyway. My world is full of clichés. My empty thinking space finds trivia to occupy itself as we trudge along the path that leads from one brown building to another. Nothing is open. We find no one. I can feel your frustration. "This is a waste of time," I mutter, and then realize the depth of my words and bite hard on my cheek.

We walk past the garden of remembrance and I see a small wooden sign pointing the way to the children's garden. It is in bad taste. Why would children want to play here? I stare. My breath catches. I understand. I look at you and see the lines of age and experience on your wasting skin, and I see the sadness in your exhausted expression. You turn away and maybe in that moment I can understand why you are *okay with this* as you keep telling me. Some things are natural and some things are not. You may be going quicker than either of us want, but you are a long way from the children's garden.

The stillness around us makes me want to cry and I'm glad to follow you back to the building. I don't want to think of the dead children. I can't think of them. It might make me drift too far. I like to think it wouldn't, but it might. *Doctor drifting.* Like before. And I don't need that right now. Right now is all about you.

We find the office. It's locked, but the small waiting room is open, so we take some leaflets advising us on coping with bereavement—just because they're there—and head out to look at the chapel. The large doors are locked and like naughty children we creep across the perfect lawn to balance between the flowers and peer into the gloom.

The window is small and modern and I can't see much apart from a couple of rows of pine pews. I don't know what I'm looking for so I step back. I don't want to look too much. It makes me think time is folding again. Here with you, but I'll soon be here again *without* you.

Your face is pressed to the glass, hands wrapped round the edges of your eyes to block out the light, but after a while you push away and nod slightly.

"What do you think?" I ask, as if we are looking at a venue for a party.

"I suppose it'll do," you say. "Seems pleasant enough."

We head back to the car and I'm relieved to start the engine and leave the place behind. Halfway home I open the window a touch. I say I'm hot. It's a lie. That awful rotting smell is erupting from you as you burp and release more liquid into the tub. I think you don't notice it. Maybe your sense of smell has decayed already. Another part of you breaking down. Irreparable. After a while I shut the window again, but it lingers on. I shallow breathe, ashamed of myself.

You are quite perky when we get home, happy to have another thing ticked from your list now that the doctor has told you, "Two months, no more." I smile and laugh as I make the tea and you think I'm fine, but it takes me hours to shake the dark shadow off. I scrub hard in the shower that night, trying to wash away the cold, clinical finality of death that stabs terror into my soul. I don't have your Zen.

After Mum left and we rented the house out—moving into the grounds of the special school you were working at—Penny and Paul used to sneak out and spy on the town embalmers. Did you ever know about that? They used to peer through the windows at the cadavers in the back room of the funeral parlor or crematorium or whatever it was. They would come back giggling and exhilarated. I pretended to be interested, but I never went with them. The coldness never fascinated me. Terrified me, perhaps, the stillness of it all, but never fascinated me. I sometimes wonder how true their breathless stories were and if in fact they ever saw a body at all, but I'm glad I never went with them. There is too much of the darkness inside me without adding to the fear. Even as a child I knew that.

I realize I'm shallow breathing again when I hear Penny release the water and send it fleeing through the pipes. I put the kettle on to make more tea.

5

"The boys are coming." We look at each other and say the words and it feels like we're speaking in metaphors. We may as well have said a hurricane was coming. It feels that way. A force of nature. A law unto itself. Fascinating and destructive. Burning itself out too soon. I blow hair out of my face. We are certainly making the house safe, in a different way than you would for a storm maybe, but still battening down the hatches.

Penny holds up a dust-coated bottle of port that usually stands on the kitchen windowsill. "How long have you had this?"

I stare and shrug. "Came with some Stilton, I think. Couple of years ago? Maybe three? We'd better hide it anyway."

She looks at the label and laughs. "Hmmm. Consume within one year of purchase. This one can go straight in the bin." She empties it into the sink, the smell very strong for a moment, and then puts the bottle in the recycling bin. The windowsill looks strange without it and for an irrational moment I want to fish it out of the bag and put it back. There has been too much change. I want it to stop. But of course nothing ever does.

Pulling two bottles of wine out of the fridge, Pen waves them at me. "Where can we hide these?"

"Under my bed?"

She nods, giggling, her eyes bright, her *glow* bright. "Good plan. We can have a liquid midnight feast later." She is halfway up the stairs when she comes dashing back and grabs the corkscrew from the drawer. "We won't get far without this!" I start laughing too and she puts it between her teeth and that nearly sends me over the edge. Penny has been through some stuff in her life. But with all that glow she is forever eighteen, bubbly and full of life. Listening to her thump up the stairs I don't even feel envious, just in awe.

More searching finds an untouched bottle of vodka left over from Christmas and half a bottle of whisky under the sink. I have no idea how they got there. We put those under my bed too and then empty the medicine cupboard on to the breakfast bar. There are two large bottles of liquid morphine—you no longer need them now you have the constant pump attached—and four trays of heart pills, sectioned into individual boxes with the names of the days on them. Penny stares at it all before pushing the pills out of sight, *out of mind*, into a carrier bag. She is in full organizational flow now. "I'll take these down to the chemist while you have a shower. I won't be long."

I ache slightly as she whisks the pills away and out of the house. One route for you is now gone. The fast, self-medicated heart attack is no longer an option. Just the slow road left. I wish I'd hidden some of your tablets where she wouldn't find them. But I didn't. I didn't think. My thinking space was too full of cliché and claptrap.

I scrub myself hard in the shower.

The twins arrive within half an hour of each other despite living hundreds of miles apart. This doesn't surprise either Penny or me. The twins have always been like that, as if they never stopped breathing in the same fluid, taking a little of the womb with them as they grew. Sometimes I think that link has hurt them far more than helped them. They feel each other's self-destruction and feed it. I don't know which boy started on that damaged road first, but they took the other with them, that much is for sure.

It's Davey who gets here first, even though he was the second-born, the youngest of the five, if only by seven minutes. Penny opens the door with a squeal of delight and I grin behind her. My dread melts away a little. It's only Davey, after all. His dark hair is too long, but the brown eyes underneath it look soft and scared and warm with no hint of rage or madness. I join in their hug, Penny tiny between us and I squeeze tight. Poor Davey. Always a boy to us.

"You're looking good, Davey," I whisper and he crushes me back, knowing what I mean. He is too thin and his clothes are cheap and tatty and he has wrinkles on his face that shouldn't be there yet. When he hesitantly smiles I can see the nicotine stains on his teeth and there is a gap where one is missing at the side. But he looks good *in the eyes*. And that's where it counts. "Do you fancy a bacon sandwich?" I hide my tears with a grin.

Unlike Penny, Davey goes straight up to see you without even taking off his jacket. When he comes back down ten minutes later he isn't crying. He doesn't say much, smoking a cigarette before eating his sandwich. I think maybe he is stronger than all of us in his own way. Penny is filling him in on all of little James's antics and he laughs. "When I'm sorted, I'll have to come up and visit you. It's about time the little lad got to know his Uncle Davey better." Penny nods, and in this minute she truly does want that to happen. We're in a bubble again, all of us together this time.

Not a bubble of time though. This time it's a bubble of self-deception.

We want so much to believe that it's easy for Davey to slip in and out of Penny's world, but deep down we all know it isn't. It isn't Penny's fault. It's Davey's. He thinks his world is normal like everyone else's, but it's been so long since he's been part of the status quo he doesn't realize how displaced he is. His world is not ours. He doesn't belong in it as we don't in his. There comes a time when the two paths no longer cross.

I wait for a pause in their to and fro of talk so I can ask him how he's doing. He shrugs. "One day at a time, Sis. You know how it is. I'm still in the sheltered accommodation for another three months. Then we'll see. I've got to be strong, haven't I? Got to keep taking the pills." He smiles and that's good. It's difficult to equate him with the screaming monster on the phone who claimed he was going to come and shoot me with a sawed-off shotgun a couple of years ago. Not that he ever had such a gun. And not that he remembers it. Or if he does, it isn't in the way that I do. And I can understand that. I was like that when I was in the dark drift.

Penny pushes the chocolate biscuits at him. "Eat those. If we eat any more of them we'll burst." He takes one diligently from the packet under the watchful gaze of his eldest sister, but he just holds it until I put the mug of tea down on the table. Penny leans forward. "And you're staying away from the drink? And the drugs?"

Davey nods. "Have to, don't I? If I want to be sane."

I watch him put four teaspoons of sugar in his tea before he stirs it. He needs to get a rush from somewhere. As if the mention of drugs is his cue, the doorbell goes and Simon is here. We are nearly all here; only Paul to come.

Penny squeals with delight all over again and the twins hug. Simon and Davey inhabit the same normality and I think it makes Davey feel more relaxed. Simon has always made Davey feel better about things, even though Simon is further along down the road than his twin. Simon is more at home in their strange lives than Davey is. Sometimes I can see Davey's longing for the real world, whatever that may be.

The kitchen is too full and even though I'm not hungry I eat a bacon sandwich. Davey has another one too, ketchup dripping down his denim shirt and giving Penny something to fuss over. She is maternal, I'll give her that. Simon asks for a sandwich, but it sits untouched on his plate. I think he's forgotten it's there. He's concentrating on his cigarette. He has arrived holding an open can of extra strong lager. Something cheap. It isn't a brand I've ever heard of and for a moment I feel as if we're in a soap opera and none of this is real. The can makes me think of it. It looks like one of those fake brands they use on the BBC.

The boys share a smile over something Penny has said and I can almost see their childish faces shimmering under the worn skin they have now. Only just, but the traces are still there. That makes me sadder than if they had been gone forever and I go to the sink and slowly wash up, hiding in the task. They don't notice, both caught up in Penny's glow, and I don't mind. It is as it is.

"Right, I'm going to see the old man." Simon stands unsteadily. He leaves the sandwich untouched, but keeps hold of the can. Penny, bless her, makes him leave his cigarette down here. She does these things with a light touch. If I had said the same thing it would have made him feel bad. Penny can do these things with a smile and a whisper and make people feel good about themselves.

Simon stays up there for longer and I wonder what sense you two are making to each other. Maybe you have become a shrine or a relic or a font of knowledge and giver of absolution now that your time is limited. I wonder if any of them see that you're just a tired old man waiting to die and I wonder at my arrogance for having that thought.

Simon is crying when he comes back downstairs, still carrying the can, and Penny tries to make it easy for him with platitudes.

"It's okay to cry, sweetheart, but Dad wouldn't want you to be sad," she says. "He'd want you to remember the good times."

Watching her soothing him makes me love her more. She may be no good at taking the hard, but she knows how to spread the easy. Simon calms down, but I can see the desolation in his dazed eyes and I know that the scared boy inside is crying for himself. Who will be on the other end of the phone for his slurred, indecipherable rambles? Who will help him find the rent when he's spent it on cheap beer and drugs? Who will speak to the council and sort out his benefits? Me? Penny? Davey?

I don't see it. Our seams will have come apart.

These things are in the future though, and for now it is all laughter and tears. I am relieved when a nurse comes. It's not Barbara and I wish it were, but at least I'm out of the kitchen. I'm tired and the loudness of everything they say hurts my ears. I wait in the hall until she comes down. She is brisk and efficient. She lacks Barbara's softness. Barbara's heart. I let her out, enjoying a moment of cold air in my smoke-sore eyes and then I go upstairs to find some peace. I seek solace at your stinking, rotting shrine.

I sit by the bed and hold your hand. You are awake, the bed professionally tidy and I see the spit jar of mouthwash has been emptied and washed. We look into each other for a moment and silently acknowledge again how well we were coping as just two. I smile, and so do you.

One shaky hand points at the cup of water, the long fingers exaggerated by the lack of flesh. You aren't able to grip it. The reality of your fast decline threatens to bring tears, but I lock them down and hold the cup for you, letting small sips drip into your withered mouth.

"I didn't think you could drink anymore. You haven't drunk anything for days."

You grunt slightly, one eyebrow raising a margin in your yellow forehead. "I thought it would make it happen quicker." The words are slow and heavy. Not in your voice. "Just made me bloody thirsty." The sound may not be yours, but the meaning is still you and I laugh, but you don't smile. You take a few more sips and then sink back into the bed, exhausted. "Thanks, darling." I don't say anything and you shut your eyes. The lids are so thin I can almost see through them. I wonder what is going on in there, in your private bubble.

Within minutes you are sleeping again, thick breaths crawling in and out of you. You look peaceful despite the fight inside. Sometimes it's easier to talk to people when they're asleep. They can't answer back and they take in your words better.

You made me read a book when I was little where they piped words into children as they slept, forming their place in society. It was a good book. It was a thinking book. I think maybe I should dig it out and read it again someday. I could use a good thinking book.

I lean forward and send my suggestion in through your ear. "The boys aren't your fault, you know." It isn't much, but you sigh, and I hope that it's made you sleep easier.

When I go back to the kitchen I can barely see my brothers through the fog of smoke and I wonder how often I've looked at them properly. Simon seems fairly lucid and for a second I see the ghost of the bright boy with the shock of blond hair who was so fit and healthy and into everything. Simon was into life when he was young. That changed somewhere along the way.

"Is Paul coming?" Simon looks around as if he expects our eldest brother to appear magically in the room. "Where is he? Haven't heard from him in a while." He thinks he is speaking clearly, but his voice slurs wildly from one word to the next and his eyes are narrower than they used to be. I'm sure it's just because he needs to concentrate to focus, but it makes him look mean. Maybe that's how you have to look to survive in his world.

His cigarette ash drops to the floor and I know with a moment's clarity that I will never see him again after this is done. I can feel the family unraveling with your life. We are disconnecting—satellites spinning outward from a broken spool.

Davey slips quietly out of the back door and I follow him into the garden. It's cold now and getting dark, but we know our way down the path to the swings, our feet as steady on the broken slabs as they always have been. I don't worry about treading on the cracks. That fear is too far in the past. Growing up is about realizing that the cracks in the pavement are nothing to worry about. It's the cracks inside that count.

Davey takes the left swing and I sit on the right. My breath dances with his smoke in the cold air and I grip the chains that feel so much smaller than they used to. The plastic U of the seat digs into the excess flesh of my thighs, reinforcing this. None of it seems to bother Davey as he smokes the cigarette right down to his fingertips while staring at the house and garden. I wonder what ghosts he's seeing.

"So. You all right, Sis?"

I'm surprised by the care in his voice and look over. His face is all shadows and flashes of white in the gloom.

"Yes—course I am. Why?" I say.

"Just wondered. I never understood why you came back here." He pauses. "No, that's not true. I understood why someone might need to go home for a while. But I don't understand why you stayed once you were back on your feet." Despite the cold, his fingers deftly roll another cigarette. "I thought you'd want to get back out there."

I think that maybe that place they keep him in has given Davey too much thinking time. In that moment, part of me wants the maniac back. "Just seemed like the sensible thing to do. I like it here." Heat rises in my face. I don't want to talk about me. I don't want to talk about me and the world *out there*. And I don't want to talk about my drifts. I'm not the one with problems. Not really.

"Davey," I ask, "what happened to Simon? How did he get into that stuff?" It's a diversionary tactic, but I do want to know. In my memories Simon goes from sixteen and normal to seventeen and wild and crazy with no gradient in-between. I know that this can't be real. I guess I just wasn't paying attention when his cracks began to show.

Davey sniffs and wipes the back of his hand across his nose before inhaling again. The scent of the roll-up tobacco is rich and comforting in the fresh air and I breathe it in.

"There was this DJ bloke that we used to hang around with . . ." I almost drift as I wonder how many sad stories start with those words: *There was this man or woman or girl or boy and for a while all was well . . .* but instead I focus hard on the glowing end of Davey's cigarette and listen.

"Simon hung there more than me. The bloke was older than us. Probably about thirty, I guess. Sometimes Simon would stay there, you know, overnight. That bloke was a bit of a hero to Simon, I think." The smoke hangs almost unmoving between us. "One time he stayed there and then after that we didn't go back again. Not once. Simon wouldn't talk about it either. Not even to me. I think the drugs started after that."

He offers me half the cigarette, but I shake my head. Smelling it is enough for me. The chains clink and squeal softly as Davey stretches backward in the seat. "I sometimes wonder why anyone ever talks at all," he says. "They never fucking say anything useful." He grins over at me and I smile back. Sometimes Davey surprises me too. He stands up, a black outline ahead of me, his big hands resting on his hips.

"Paul should be here soon. That'll be odd, all of us back in the old house again." He wanders inside and I say I'll follow in a minute. I look up at your window, bright in the darkness, and I can see myself on the other side of it. Here and there at once. Time folding again.

6

I see it for the second time just after I buy the house from you. I am twenty-five. I am broken. You have trekked off to Nepal declaring no need for physical possessions, just as you declare that you no longer have a need for alcohol. Nepal is a long way to go to get away from hard liquor, but you are determined to leave it behind and get addicted to Zen. You say it's less harmful for your liver than vodka. I manage a smile as we agree a figure and say our goodbyes. You don't ask why I would want to buy the house. You are too busy fighting your own demons to see mine and I can forgive you that. I am not good at sharing the deep things. I guess that's why I've left it all until now.

The sale goes through quickly and I put the money in a building society for you and distribute the rest out to each child-satellite for an early inheritance as you requested. It doesn't take long for it to be gone and wasted. At least I have the bricks and mortar to show for it.

When you drift—especially like I did—you need an anchor. You need something that you belong with and that belongs to you, and I have nothing else. Everything that was solid is gone. Even you have left me for the goats, mountains, prayers and dysentery of a mystic land.

I don't know it then—I'm too dark in the drift—but we are all deconstructing. The boys are in London and you think they're just being young and wild and angry at you for the whole Shetland experience, but they are in fact starting the degeneration that will have fully set in by the time you come back. It won't be long before their landlady kicks them out, starting a lifetime habit, and as with all the landlords that follow, no one will blame her. Not even Davey and Simon themselves.

Penny is living what I choose to imagine is a fabulous and glamorous existence on some Costa or other. It later turns out that she has her share of problems, but, as I stand in the small room, I can't see that her life would be anything other than perfect. And Paul? I never really know what's going on with Paul. As I stand in the back room peering out of the window I don't even know where he is. He either answers his phone or he doesn't. And I'm not much in the mood for talking. The words have all dried up at the back of my throat. On a subconscious level I have come home to fade because I can't see where else this bleakness can lead. And I want to be left alone while I do it. There has been too much talk. Even my own words barely make sense.

I know that I could go to Penny and she would welcome me with open, glowing arms, but I wouldn't fit there. I don't think I fit anywhere but here. Here is safe. Here I don't have to face my broken marriage and my broken heart or what's left of my broken mind that the pills are fighting so valiantly to repair. Here I can breathe and let the cracks show. And maybe bleed through them a little.

I peer out through the curtain and the sun is shining brightly, glinting on the chains of the swings. I can feel it on my skin through the glass. It feels good because the house has that coldness buildings get when they have been empty for too long. The heating will be on for days before it manages to breathe any life back into the walls. I can hear the boiler raging. I think it will take more energy than it can produce to warm me. I can barely feel my insides most days. I stare out through the glass for a little longer before turning to face the remnants of the room that Penny and I used to share.

It's the same, but not. I can see that you have been distracted by the changes in your life. Like you, the dimensions of the room have stayed the same, but the contents have changed a little. It's odd, a bit like adjusting to the new you. You are sober, but still compulsive as you seek answers for the failed marriages and the years lost in an alcoholic haze. Eventually you'll leave the questions behind, but not yet. I trace my finger on a windowsill that feels almost damp.

Parts of the room are gone. The small beds we occupied have been dismantled long ago and you have replaced them with a desk and a small lamp. The room is obviously intended to be a study of sorts. There are boxes of paper everywhere, notes in your sharp scribble covering sheets and sheets of it. Beside the desk, the waste-paper basket is full of crumpled, abandoned balled-up paper. I think about reading some of the words, but my brain doesn't have room for them—all the hurt and empty space fills it. Instead I just stare at it all for a minute or two before turning away.

Our old bookshelf still stands in the corner; badly drawn flowers covering the sides in felt tip, their brightness faded with too many years passed. I can still remember drawing them, sharp and clear. Mine are small tight squiggles on stalks and Penny's have big green leaves and huge petals. Make from that what you will. It's not rocket science.

Dusty children's books still sit in a raggedy heap on the shelves. I wonder why you haven't boxed them up or given them to a charity. Maybe you were planning to, but all the writing on those screwed up pieces of paper got in the way. You are like Paul in that way. Obsessive about things.

I pick up a large white hardback. Some of the shiny
spine has been ripped away exposing the thin cream-
colored mulchy cardboard underneath. I look at the front
and the bright picture rings bells in my head. This was a
loved book. Maybe that's why you haven't packed them
away yet. Maybe these books keep us with you even when
we're far away. Talismans. Unlike our mother, you love us
better as children than as babies.

I rub the thick seventies paper between my fingers,
memories of smell and taste and sound filling my head—
here and just out of reach—and I flick to the first story.
It's a fairy tale of course: a princess and her equally beautiful partner dance across a glittering ballroom beneath an
ornate title, leaving no question about the ending. I don't
remember it ever spoiling my enjoyment of the stories. I
still believed in happy endings back then. Even after Mum
left, a little sparkle still lived inside me. Children recover
well from things like that, don't they? The picture sends a
hum through me and the book feels familiar. On the next
page the story starts to tell itself and I wonder how many
years have passed since it's had that chance. The letters are
large and black and tug at my insides. *Once upon a time there
was a beautiful princess in a faraway land.*

My hand trembles. I feel as if my skin is shaking itself free
from my flesh and then the pages blur. I used to love these
stories. I hug the book tight and lean against the window,
huge sobs escaping from my hollow chest. I slide to the

floor, the windowsill banging hard into my spine. I don't care. The pain is outside of me. I am empty. I am nothing. I can't hold it together anymore, pills or no pills. There is too much darkness at the edge of my vision and I'm tired of fighting it. The drift has me. The drift has always had me. I was just too stupid to know. My eyes glaze and the book slips from my hand.

There was this girl, you see.

And there was this man.

And for a while, all was well.

I go to London when I'm twenty. Everyone has left home and I feel like the world is passing me by and taking opportunities with it. That's what Penny tells me anyway, carrying me along with her excitement and glow and the rush of her words in the phone. She loves London. I'll love it too. She has no doubt about this and before I can breathe properly I've packed my suitcase and I'm on the train, eyes wide and twitchy like a rabbit, a bundle of nerves and excitement.

Penny has a little flat in East Ham and she's right. I do love it. We laugh a lot in those first two months, spending our evenings drinking cheap wine and smoking Benson & Hedges. I'm temping in an office, answering phones and typing letters; she is selling expensive makeup in Selfridges. She is very good at it, selling things. Customers like to buy from people with the glow, as if they think that personal shine will come with the product. It doesn't, of course. If it did I'd be first in the queue. But I've been around Penny long enough to know that the glow just clings to the individual. You can't share it.

We are young and Penny has a lot of boyfriends. Men like Penny, they always have. I don't know how she keeps track of her admirers though, because the phone that sits on the table in the small hallway isn't plugged in. Penny polishes the ivory and gilt pretty much every day, making sure it shines and shows off its worth, but it remains silent. We could plug it in, but there would be no point, we can't afford the line rental. Penny has no intention of getting us connected and never has.

I ask her why she bought the phone in the first place if she wasn't going to be able to use it and she looks at me like I'm mad. "People will think we're poor if we don't have a phone," is her explanation. It makes me laugh, but she is serious. She knows the importance of appearance, does Penny.

Sometimes we see Paul. He's living just outside London and occasionally turns up with a bottle of wine and stories of his endeavors that make me laugh until I cry, Penny squealing beside me. If I hear stories like Paul's from other people I take them with a pinch of salt. With Paul, though, I know that, however unlikely they may be, they are true. Paul is in many ways larger than life. He dominates conversations and social events, finding childlike fun in everything. This doesn't always go down well with others, especially when his dominating becomes domineering.

Mostly though, when in public, he entertains. He makes people smile and that makes him happy and the audience either falls in love with him or at least begrudgingly admires him. When things are working for him, Paul is around. But then he disappears for months at a time and I know that, under the funny, Paul doesn't find life all that easy. He's stuck between me and Penny: too much hard and too much easy fighting inside him. Maybe that's why, like you, he drinks too much and smokes too much. Maybe that's his way out of the drift. He drives fast cars and earns silly sums of money, but nothing is stable around him. He spends more than he earns with a desperation that I think most people can't see. I can, though. Even at barely twenty I can see. Still, you can't tell Paul. No one can. And despite it all I love him and begrudgingly admire him.

I have boyfriends too. I don't glow like Penny, but I am tall and slim and my sandy hair falls to my shoulders and when we go out together we look good—different enough, but both shining with youth. We often double-date, but there is nothing serious going on under the warmth of the wine and the man's touch. Not for either of us.

Until that moment when, out of the blue, it happens. I meet him.

The One.

Whatever.

I often wonder how things would've been if we'd gone to a different bar or just gone home, but playing "what if" games with the events of your life is a road to madness and I don't need any more of those. My head is a network of those paths that I can see when I shut my eyes. What is, is. What was, was.

He doesn't speak to Penny as we push our way to the bar, my sister already peering around for some willing male volunteer to buy the drinks we can't afford to buy for ourselves. He smiles straight at me. His teeth are white. I notice that. His smile is wide and his eyes twinkle under his dark hair. I smile back, the bar, the drink and even Penny forgotten.

"Hi," he says.

"Hi," I say, right back. I fall in love in a snap. I can almost hear it inside. Within two months we are living in his large house in Notting Hill. I have a golden ring on my finger which proves his promise of unending love. I am the fairy-tale princess and have my fairy-tale ending. And all in that snap.

A year or so later, the snaps I hear are different. More varied. Subtle variations on a theme. I can hear the sharp snap in the air when his mood changes suddenly. I can feel the tension that grips my shoulders and my gut. *What now?* the pang asks. What did I say wrong? Did I put the cans in the cupboard unevenly? Is the TV remote control slightly out of place on the table? Or is it just one of those days?

Onomatopoeia is the key to my existence during my married years. *Snap. Crack. Slap. Bang*: sounds that belong in comic books rather than in my world. There's no Superman to come and save me, though. My battle is quieter and more pathetic than that. The kind you just have to get on with on your own.

Some of the sounds I like. The click of the front door as it shuts behind him when he goes to work. The gasp of held air I can release when the house is my own. I don't relax though. Never—not entirely. Since I no longer work, he schedules my day for me. There is cleaning and shopping and cooking and ironing. Sometimes I get things done quickly and try to watch a film or read a magazine on the sofa, but it makes my stomach knot too much to enjoy. He rings every hour to make sure everything is as it should be and sometimes he comes home early to surprise me.

I don't think he'd like to find me with my feet up, reading something pithy about hair and makeup and the lives of celebrities. In fact, I know he wouldn't like it. Reading isn't something he likes me to do. He can't share in reading. It can only be in my head and try as he might he can't get all the way in there. That's part of what will make me take the job in the library, years later. A way-too-late kick in the balls to someone long ago left behind.

I don't know exactly when he starts to show himself through his cracks. Not long after we are married, maybe two or three months. I am sitting on one of the huge leather sofas that fill our expensive lounge, hanging up the phone after a long girly chat with Penny and then I jump out of my seat with the smack as the remote control hits the wall beside me. I stare at him, confused. I can't believe that he threw it. Not at me, not then, but that he threw it at all.

"I was watching the film," he says. "I couldn't hear it over your pointless drivel and now I don't have a clue what is happening." He is calm but his words are sharp and cold and I stare at him, my heart pounding hard, my face hot.

"Sorry," I mumble.

"Only call your sister once a week from now on." He turns his head back to the TV. We sit in silence and with a cold dread I feel the paper walls of my castle crumple and sag.

Most things in life change gradually. Events creep up on you from behind just like the language. You barely notice the beginnings; it's only when things go terribly wrong that we wipe the sleep from our eyes and wail miserably, "How the hell did that happen?" Still, that's the way for all of us. Even you with your Zen and your calm intelligence. You brush off and put aside the first symptoms of the cancer that is killing you. *It's just a touch of indigestion*, that's what you think. *Nothing to worry about.*

I am like that with the malignancy in my marriage. The first few symptoms of my fairy-tale prince's very flawed character are easy to brush aside. After a few cautious, watchful days of everything going back to normal, I put the remote-control incident into a box in my head where I don't have to think about it. He must have just had a bad day at work. This is what I tell myself when I lie awake in the warmth of our bed, listening to the gentle sounds of his breath as he sleeps. Neither of us mentions it. I don't mention it to Penny either and I tell myself that's because it's not worth mentioning, despite the faint echo of alarm bells ringing in my subconscious. I don't want to tell Penny, that's the truth of it. I think she will be disappointed in me, or worse, maybe she will be expecting it, because it is all too good to be true.

Three months later I can no longer ignore the symptoms.

He comes to pick me up from the office and I come out laughing with a male colleague. I don't know why we're laughing, probably just a small, polite joke shared in a lift by two people who barely know each other. My smile falls when I get into the car and see his face. The tires screech.

He doesn't speak for two days other than to call the agency and tell them I won't be coming back to work. I cry a lot. I ask him what I've done. He pins me down on the bed, straddling me, his knees on my arms. Leaning forward he spits in my face, his hands on my face, fingers pressing into my eyes. His words assault me until his rage passes and then he cries himself. I shake inside as he retreats into a ball in the corner. I feel sorry for him. I feel sorry for me. He seems so vulnerable and I sit on the carpet too and wrap my bruised arms around him.

"Hush," I say. "It'll be all right. We'll be all right. I don't care about work. I won't go anymore. I just care about you. About us."

I think I can mend him. This is my mistake because he's not broken, he's just been put together wrong. The only breakable thing in the relationship is me.

I live in a drift, not a deep one, but a dark one, and I save whatever shine I can muster for when Penny and Paul come and visit, which isn't as often as they'd like, especially Penny, but more than enough for me to cope with. I live on a wire and the stress of visitors is enough to send me over the edge. They add an unknown quantity to my day. I can never judge what they might say or do, or what I may say or do in a brief relaxed moment that may need to be paid for later. I avoid drinking when we have visitors. I need to keep my wits about me. I'm good at pretending, though. I don't think anyone notices. My brother and sister are far too busy being happy for me.

I watch him talk with them as we laugh over wine and more of Paul's tall stories and I wonder how they don't see me flinch when he casually rests his hand around my shoulders. The hand that has pushed and pulled and squeezed and punched me. I try to remember that it has also loved, but just like the ring that doesn't fit my thinned finger anymore, the idea of love has long since disappeared. There is something going on between us, but it isn't love.

Time passes in gray waves and I have no real concept of it outside of hourly telephone calls, bruises, insults and terrifying moments of affection. I have closed down. There is me and him and I can't give attention to anyone else. It's too exhausting. Penny goes to Turkey to live on a boat with a man she has met, and Paul disappears. I don't worry about Paul and I doubt Penny does. We understand. Another business has gone bust and he is hiding.

Paul owes him money, though. Not a large amount, and I never even knew about the loan, but it's great fight ammunition. How my family are a drain on him. Just like me.

I don't see Paul for two years. Like Penny, he prefers things easy, and out of sight is out of mind. He doesn't like to look at things that make him feel bad, but then you know that already. You don't see him much either and I figure he owes you money, too. You have come back from the Shetlands, admitting defeat on your second attempt at marriage, determined to clean up and I fob you off. I know it upsets you, but I need to live my insanity in peace. I'm sorry, Dad.

Then things change again. My eyes constantly burn with exhaustion. I don't sleep much anymore and that's probably why, once again, I don't notice the early symptoms. I'm too preoccupied with surviving day to day and telling myself that things aren't that bad to realize that a little thing like a period has gone missing.

I am at the counter in Waitrose when I suddenly feel sick, badly sick, dizzy and queasy like the first attack in a dangerous case of food poisoning. I leave my basket and dash into the toilets. I am sure I am going to throw up. My skin sweats cold and I throw handfuls of water on to my face before sitting heavily on a toilet seat, locking the cubicle behind me. I hug the cistern, not caring about any germs, enjoying the cold ceramic. Dark spots gather in the corners of my vision and the world swims slightly as I fight to control the nausea. I can't be sick. I don't want to be sick. I have to get home before the next phone call.

I sit very still for ten minutes or so and then trust myself enough to stand. The worst of it has passed, only a clingy wet feeling is left in my gut and my mouth tastes stale. Ignoring the strange looks that must be coming my way I collect my basket and pay. I need to get home.

At eight o'clock the next morning I am dry-heaving over the kitchen sink, the sickness grabbing me too quickly to get to the toilet. He stares at me, putting down his toast.

"Maybe you should go to the doctor," he suggests quietly.

"I'll be all right," I say. "It's probably just a bug."

He nods and hands me some kitchen roll to wipe the saliva from my mouth. The doctor can be tricky. I only go if I really have to because I just can't be sure of the reaction.

A doctor, like a book, is out of his control. He can't be sure of what I might say within those private walls.

I don't go to the doctor, I just fight the queasiness for a couple of days, but he can see that I'm doing it. I see him watching me. That causes more sharp twists in my gut that don't help the nausea to fade. I wait for a reaction, but there is no sign of his loss of patience. He smiles at me and strokes my hair as we watch TV. I wonder what is coming, but there is only more tenderness. It sets my nerves on edge and I can't sleep.

He brings home a pregnancy test and waits outside the bathroom chewing on a fingernail. He smiles at the fact I hadn't thought of this and as he patronizes me I grit my teeth and read the instructions. When I come out and show him the definite blue line, he laughs like he did in the beginning and kisses me all over.

I relax slightly. Maybe things will be better when there are three of us. For the first time in a long time I feel the fizz of excitement. In fact, it's the first time in a long time that I've felt anything at all.

I sleep with a hand on my belly and when we go to the doctor, we go together. All smiles.

Leopards don't change their spots. Another cliché to fill my empty thinking space. I'm lying at the bottom of the stairs, the pain not quite gripping me fully, too shocked to feel and I'm angry at myself for my stupidity, for not realizing. For still wanting to believe in fairy-tale endings, when I know they don't exist. For not getting my shit together and getting out of there.

Unmoving, I can see red spreading outward through the fibers of our thick cream carpet and I feel the first wave of panic. I think that maybe I blacked out for a couple of seconds because somewhere behind me I can hear him calling an ambulance. My head is foggy. This can't be good, I think, if he's getting a doctor.

I try to move, but I can't. When you're seven months pregnant moving isn't easy at the best of times, and when you've just been shoved down the stairs it's another matter. Or tripped down the stairs, or walked into a cupboard, or whatever else he's going to tell them so convincingly that he'll end up believing it himself.

I almost laugh. I hate myself. I can see my heeled shoe on the floor beside me. It has come off as I've tumbled. The red is creeping toward it and it's trying to tell me something but I don't want to listen. Not yet. My chest hurts from where he slammed his knee into it only minutes ago. Something cracked in there. I'm sure of it.

I can hear him crying. I hate him almost as much as I hate me. His words are slurring into the phone. He's drunk. That'll be his excuse when he begs me to forgive him. He was drunk and I laughed a little too loudly at something his partner had said over dinner and *why the hell was a pregnant woman wearing so much makeup anyway?*

I look at the shoe and the blood and know there won't be a next time. I'll either die tonight or leave him and, from my place on the carpet, it feels like fifty-fifty. I don't realize that dying is not as easy as people presume.

As something shifts badly inside and the terrible pain starts in my belly, I know that as usual I've left things too late. My weakness is killing my baby. I scream, but not from the pain. Awful as that is, the scream comes from somewhere else, for something else and someone else. Someone I'm never going to know.

In the distance I can hear the wail of the ambulance, but I no longer care. I should have seen that blue line and walked right out of the house. But I didn't. Of course I didn't. Squeezing my eyes shut, unable to ignore the blood anymore, I cross my heart and hope to die.

I don't, of course. Wishes and fairy tales don't come true.

I am in the hospital for a couple of weeks. I give birth to my baby, but she's already dead. She's gone straight from the A of life to the Z of it, without any of the ups and downs and shapes of the letters in-between. I landed badly and her tiny neck snapped and her skull was damaged. She was dead before we left the house.

They clean me out with brisk efficiency, adding to the hollowness inside me. I wonder if they've taken my organs out with her. It certainly feels like it. I am an empty balloon and there is nothing that can breathe air into me.

He comes to see me and realizes that it's all over. He is afraid, which surprises me. It diminishes him and I hate that someone so small has caused all this pain.

"I want a divorce," I hear myself saying.

"Are you going to go to the police? About the . . . accident?"

I stare at him for a long time, his self-concern etched into his shallow face and I wish I could have seen this clearly on all the other days. Like I see now. Right through the cracks.

We agree a deal. I want to buy your house. It's all that will stay in my head without wriggling out. I want to go home. And I want him to pay for it. I want him to pay for a lot of things, but I don't have the energy for that so I take what's easiest for him to give. Money.

He doesn't argue. He can't. He nods numbly. He has too much to lose. Not like me—I've already lost everything. There will be no more babies. The doctor was quite clear on that.

After I've signed the papers, after I see the relief in his weak and broken face, I sink back into the drift that's been waiting impatiently for me and I let the pain take over. I hear the doctors whispering. They talk about pills and rest homes. I push myself further into the bed. The pillow is soft. I wonder how it would feel over my face. Not too bad, I imagine. Not compared with this.

I go into the drift for a long time. From somewhere inside I know there are people looking after me and I wish they would stop. They insistently drag me back to the world with their talking and medication and care. Eventually I can't fight them any longer and let them bring me round to not-quite-normal. It's a couple of months, however, before they let me leave and I can feel their eyes on me, wondering how long it will be before I return. The drift is like that. It never really lets you go. And they know that.

I go straight home and buy your house, ready to fade away in it, and so the new chapter begins. I go into the bedroom. I find the fairy tale book. It tears at my heart and I drift a little.

I come out of the drift slumped against the windowsill, the fairy tale book discarded on the floor. I can just about make out the white of its worn cover. The cold fills me and I shiver, only vaguely confused at the loss of time. I'm used to these things now. The world is often disjointed at the edge of a drift. My eyes slowly adjust to the gloom. They feel sore and gritty from crying. I rub them.

The room is dark with only the street lamp glow creating shadows in the corners. At first I think I can hear her ghostly second heartbeat inside me, and all those others that will never have the chance to be. I listen to it and wonder if at last I'm truly slipping from drifter to madness, and then, as the sound grows louder, I realize that it's hoof beats I can hear, hoof beats pummeling hard into tarmac, heavy and angry. The kind of angry gallop that could leave the road chipped and damaged no matter how strong the tar. Its roar fills my ears and it stops outside the house and I think I can feel the wall tremble behind me from the blast of its voice and hot breath.

I raise my head slightly and stare at the wall. The street-light filtering in from outside has created a silhouette movie on it. Even though the beat of hooves has stopped I can still feel the throb of energy pumping through the floor.

Ignoring the logic that I am too high in the house for such a thing to be possible, a shadow on the wall rises up on its hind legs. It is magnificent and I hold my breath in wonder as that matted mane shakes angrily in outline. My eyes don't hurt now, the grit in them gone. I watch for a long time as the shape dances and twists on the wall, whirling into a blur of blackness. Occasionally, I catch the glitter of a red eye.

My body is stiff from holding one position for so long and I turn carefully around, each movement an effort, until my fingers are gripping the sill and my eyes and nose can peer over the ledge. I wipe the glass where my breath fogs it. The creature is standing in the center of the empty road, just as it was all those years ago. This time, though, despite the shadow on the wall, it is still: totally and completely still, as if it is outside of time and the world around us. There is no impatience in those heavy hooves. I take it in. I think the gnarled root that protrudes from its vast head has become more twisted, more empty of color over the years, but the solidity and sheer strength of the beast is unchanged.

There is no laughter in its red eyes as that dark head looks up at me. There is a wind outside, but the stillness it holds as the trees sway is perfect. Statuesque. I stare. I know that on the wall behind me it is still whirling madly, but I know that the dance is coming to an end. Below me there is only calm and serenity. Its presence fills the street and fills me. My stomach swells out from the hollow. I can feel my organs again.

We stare at each other through the glass and although I still know, deep down in the core of me, that we belong together, I feel no urge to run down and clamber on to its rough back. The longing is there, yes, but no urge. I don't have the energy. I think it knows this. I think I see under-standing in those red, inhuman eyes.

I sit this way, staring out and time passes. I don't know how many hours our eyes are locked, but I am aware of the moon creeping upward behind the frozen beast. I could sit like this forever, however long that may turn out to be.

Eventually it breaks our gaze and turns, energy once more unleashed, and loses itself in the field, disappearing into the night. I feel its loss and I cry some more. But I don't drift. These tears are hot and wet and I feel every one of them. I finally pull myself to my feet, ignoring the cramps and pins and needles that scream from my extremities, and go downstairs to make a cup of tea. I taste for the first time in a long time.

The next day I pack up the children's books and put them in the loft. I am still sad, but the dark drift is over.

"Paul's here," Penny calls out, her head peering round the kitchen door. I can see the steam of her breath escaping as her sharp voice breaks my spell. I jump a little as I come back to the here and now.

"I'm coming," I answer, releasing my hips from the grip of the swing. I take one last look up at your window and my fingers absently trace the outline of the dent in my chest. I smile a little.

I may only have come home, Dad, but I've come a long way since my married days, I really have.

7

It feels warm and humid in the kitchen after being in the clear, crisp air outside and I can feel my cheeks burning. There is a throb of energy at the heart of the family as we laugh and hug. I glance at the clock on the wall and am surprised to see that it is nearly seven. Time has flown away from me again. Paul is tipping a Chinese takeaway on to a plate and he grins at me in his helpless charming way under his cropped hair. I preferred it when it was longer. It was more him. He wiggles an eyebrow at his plate.

"I thought you'd all have eaten. I only got enough for one."

"It doesn't matter, darling." Penny smiles at him. "I'm making bolognese."

She will forgive him anything. I feel redundant in my kitchen and so, even though dinner isn't nearly ready yet, I begin to lay the table while Paul eats. He doesn't go upstairs. He distracts us from that by dazzling us and making us laugh.

Whereas the twins are tall and would be broad if they ever got their lives sorted out, Paul is like Penny, shorter and darker. He is a chameleon, Paul. With every failure, he reinvents himself. He has reinvented himself a lot. The thought is unkind and I try to push it away, but it rings true. I envy Paul's easy, in some ways more than Penny's. Penny can never quite put things out of sight, out of mind. Penny's easy doesn't impact people's lives the way Paul's does. I never told him how I paid in so many ways for his loan during my marriage. I don't see the point because he wouldn't get it. And maybe he'd be right. After all, even I didn't know I'd married damaged goods until it was too late, so how was he supposed to? I know I'd be the one who ended up feeling bad, wondering how the hell it happened.

Still, he is my brother and I love him. I can keep my honesty to myself. I get knives and forks out of the drawer and start laying places at the long wooden table.

"So, what are you doing these days?" I ask. "Penny says you're doing a college course or something?" Paul's life is still a mystery to us. Not long ago he was married and living in a big suburban house and doing well—maybe too well. He disappeared under the radar and then a year later he was divorced and sharing a house with a younger girl-friend and her ex-university housemates. There's a story there and I doubt it's a happy one.

He nods. "Art and design. I've brought my portfolio to show you. I'm doing some really exciting stuff at the moment."

I smile at him. It had to be something arty. That would explain the new look. Gone are the expensive suits and sharp shirts of his entrepreneur days and in are the hip and prob-ably equally expensive jeans and thin jumpers. He has a scarf round his neck. He's forty-five. I want to tell him to grow up. I want to tell him a lot of things. But I don't. Luckily there is no wine tonight because of the boys, otherwise who knows what would be said. It's that kind of night. The cracks in our family may not be showing, but we all know they're there.

I don't look at the pictures he wows the boys with. I know they will be good, but nothing original. Art isn't him. The suits were him. If I thought he would listen I would tell him that he is a good businessman. All he has to do is spend less money and care less what the world thinks of his car. I almost giggle but manage to contain myself. And they think I'm the one lost in my own world. I guess sometimes you have to hide from the world to see it properly.

I make a cup of tea while I wait for dinner to be ready. Paul and Penny are already exchanging grins that I don't understand and the boys have gone into the lounge to watch some TV. I can hear their childlike laughter coming up the hall. Everything is back as it was when we were children. The two above and the two below and me, stuck in the middle with you. The tune fills my head. *Clowns to the left of me, Jokers to the right, here I am* . . . More clutter in my head. I wonder if you like that song. I wonder how many songs you have loved and how, even if I happen upon one on the radio in a day or a month or a year from now, I will never know. I want to run upstairs and shake you awake and force you to tell me. But there isn't enough time for you to tell me everything I want to know and, as well as the drumming of hooves and the ticking clock, I can hear a part of me breaking inside as I take another small step toward accepting your loss. I feel guilty and ashamed. I don't want to let you go.

The nurses come and I watch as they ignore the smell that clings to you and plump your pillows and change your morphine driver. There are two of them. They're the night shift. The graveyard shift. The word makes me shiver as I look at the husk of you. Your hands are twitching and trembling even though you are lost somewhere in sleep or unconsciousness or wherever your mind has taken you.

"Has he got a wash booked in for tomorrow?" The taller nurse is checking the folder.

"No," I say. "He didn't want one. I'll ask him in the morning and call through if he's changed his mind."

She sniffs. "He should have a wash."

I don't like her. "If he wants a wash I'll make sure he gets one. If he doesn't want a wash then I'll make sure he doesn't get one."

I like the slight widening of her eyes. That's her told. If you were awake and here, you'd smile at that. I may not be steel all the way through, but there's a little bit in there, enough to deal with other people who should know better. The nurses leave quickly after that and I make a mental note to mention them to Barbara tomorrow. My back stays a little hunched until I hear their car disappearing down the road and then I allow myself a smile of victory.

I keep it to myself as we eat dinner. All I say is that you are still asleep. Even though he's not eating, Paul still doesn't go upstairs. I forgive him this because his job is to keep an eye on the boys and so far he's doing that. They adore him. They always have. He doesn't have Penny's glow, but he has charisma.

Despite Penny overloading his plate, Simon's spaghetti remains mostly untouched, but Davey makes a valiant effort. I clear my plate and eat several slices of garlic bread. I wonder what I can find for pudding. No wonder the swing was tight on my hips. Still, eating beats talking and I'm content to sit and listen to more of Paul's tales and I can't help but laugh along with the rest. I wish you were awake to hear our laughter.

The moon is getting high outside when we clear away the debris of our meal, tiredness finally creeping in. We're quieter. Even Penny has lost some of her glow now that the giggles are fading. It's hard not to think about what's happening to you once night has fallen and conversation dried up. We can feel each other's hard edges as we wash and scrub the surfaces and load the dishwasher.

"Me and Simon are going for a walk. We need some fresh air. You know how it is." Davey already has his coat on and Simon is clumsily trying to get his trainers done up. I'm not sure how wise it is for them to be staggering round the countryside in the dark, but they're grown men and I don't have the energy or will to stop them. These are unusual times. They're losing you.

"Okay, just be careful. That road is pitch-black at night. Keep in at the side hedges."

Davey rolls his eyes at his brother and smiles. "I think she's forgotten we used to live here."

I throw a tea towel at him. "Yes, you did, but you were more grown-up then!"

Simon giggles as he struggles with his second shoe and looks up. "She may have a point there, Bruv."

They start to laugh. They're still laughing when we wave them off down the drive. I guess sometimes you've got to see the funny side.

Back inside, the house feels emptier and I can breathe a little better. Penny and Paul are out on the swings and I finish up the cleaning and then sit in front of the TV, staring at it for an hour or so, watching the people go back and forth but not listening to a word they're saying.

At about ten, Paul goes upstairs for a brief moment and then comes back down crying. Penny hugs him. I want to, but find I just can't. I don't know why. When his eyes are dry, he lights a cigarette and stares at the wall.

"I'll have to head off soon," he says.

I stare at him, not sure I heard correctly. "You'll what?"

He looks at his watch. There is a big clock right in front of him on the wall. Why does he need to look at his watch? "I've got to get back to Manchester. Ellie's expecting me and I've got some work on tomorrow that I can't afford to miss. I need the money."

His words are coming out fast and I'm sure he's convincing himself that they're true as each one hits the air. I look at Penny. She shrugs.

"Dad's dying," I say.

He glances at me. "I've made my peace with him. I made it when he came to stay that weekend a while back. He knows that."

I want to punch him in his sanctimonious face and see if my big brother is still somewhere underneath the surface or whether this arsehole has swallowed him whole. I want to shake him and tell him it's okay to be afraid, and that we're all afraid, but we still need him here.

"But the boys," I hiss quietly. "You told Penny you'd stay over to keep an eye on the boys."

Penny is chewing one of her plumped-up lips. She doesn't like confrontation. I wonder if she'll find something to start cleaning in her panic.

"The boys will be fine. They're better than I've seen them in years." He's grabbing at his coat and car keys. There is no laughter now, no tall tales, just a man who can't deal with losing his father. Or maybe can't deal with the *process* of losing his father. I wish he could get a glimpse of other people and see that they feel and think, just like he does. Maybe then he'd realize that none of us can deal with it. We just have to suck it up and get on with it.

"The boys are great," I sigh. "The boys are lovely. But Simon could fall asleep with a cigarette going and burn the house down while we sleep."

"He won't do that. I've told him not to smoke in the lounge."

I raise an eyebrow. "Oh, that will do it then."

He stares at me. "I'll do my best to come back tomorrow. I promise. And then I'll stay over."

And the thing is, he believes it. I laugh. I hear it fill the kitchen and it isn't a pretty sound, but I can't stop myself. Somewhere the laughter turns to shouting and the words come out in a stream. I don't know what they are, but I know they're angry and mean and hurtful and they're making my face and heart burn as they escape in a torrent. Maybe in my head they're home truths. Maybe as they escape they turn into something else, something savage and nasty. Still, I don't hear the meaning in them and I feel better when they are out.

The kitchen is silent when I finish and my face cools. Penny is staring at me, her mouth open slightly. Paul has clenched his jaw. Whatever I have said, he is in the process of using it to justify his escape. He doesn't speak, just turns and leaves. I run to the door after him and scream out of it, "Remind me to do the same for you one day!" These words I hear. They tear out of my throat.

I go back inside to find Penny scrubbing the draining board. She looks up and I'm surprised to see concern in her eyes. They're searching me. It makes me feel uncomfortable. I smile a little, but that makes her look more nervous. She puts the scourer down. "Are you sure you're okay, darling? That stuff you just said . . ." She shrugs. "It wasn't called for."

"He'll get over it," I say. My mind is blank. Whatever I said couldn't have been that bad. Surely. I dig deeper but there is nothing apart from a vague memory of rage. I shrug it away. It's done and Paul is gone. And anyway, he'll get over it. Paul always does. I eat the last piece of cold garlic bread from the plate.

* * *

It is a dark night, inside and out, forcing the argument to be quickly forgotten. The boys come back at about eleven, their faces red from the air and still laughing, and they take Paul's absence in their stride with no surprise, almost as if they already knew he wouldn't be here when they returned. I curse him again, but keep it on the inside. They wouldn't understand my anger. They adore him too much for that.

I dig out some blankets for Simon and Davey and they settle down on the two sofas, the TV for company. They are in high spirits. I lean in to kiss them each goodnight as if they are still tiny boys, all clean and warm and snug in pajamas.

"Make sure you only smoke in the kitchen." I speak to both of them, but my eyes linger on Davey's. He gets the message. Simon is the brighter one, but Davey could always read between the lines.

Penny comes out of the bathroom, her face shining even after she's scrubbed her makeup off. I don't think she could switch that glow off even if she wanted to. That's how I know she will always be all right, regardless of what befalls her. People like the glow.

She has her pajamas on and her hair is pulled back in a ponytail. "Goodnight, darling. I'm going straight to bed. I'm shattered." She hugs and kisses me and wanders to the spare bedroom. I think about the two bottles of wine under my bed. I think about our giggles of earlier in the day. Maybe I did go too far with Paul. My head feels a little fuzzy, but drenching it in cold water in the bathroom sink clears it. Penny will be fine in the morning, whatever I said. She'll put it away because she won't want to think about it.

I go into my room but the TV is too loud downstairs and I stare up at the ceiling. Sleep evades me and I don't want to take anything to help send me off in case the boys really do set the house on fire. I'm funny like that. Once an idea is in my head I can't shift it and part of me is firmly convinced that we will all go up in a boy-induced blaze tonight.

Eventually, with a big sigh, I grab my dressing gown and creep out of my bed and along the corridor. I can still hear the boys talking downstairs in the kitchen. They're getting louder. Or maybe it's just that the house is quieter. I seek refuge in your room and curl up in your armchair. Your breath rattles now, but it's steady and even, the pauses between each inhale no cause yet for concern, but I wonder how your body is sustaining itself. You've shrunk so much I can't make out your form under the duvet and your arm on top of the cover is stick thin. I've heard that phrase so many times but this is the first time I've really understood the metaphor.

The clock ticks. I wonder how your heart is ticking away without the medicine. I know that you're bored of this and just want it over. I sigh. I'm glad the little light is still on, shedding some warmth in the stinking room.

I won't sleep, I think, as I stare at that unfamiliar arm, but before long my eyes close . . .

They open quickly from the doze to see you sitting on the edge of the bed, staring at me and muttering to yourself.

"Dad?"

You don't answer, you don't even hear me, your head shaking a little on your fragile neck. One arm comes up as if you're trying to point at the wall.

"What is it, Dad?" I ask you. "Do you need something? Do you need the toilet?"

I crouch in front of the bed, but you're not hearing me. You're not lucid. I don't know where you are. You sit like this, your arms waving slightly, head trembling, mouth slightly open and I'm convinced you're going to try to stand.

I hold your shoulders and try to negotiate you back into bed and although you don't fight me, you don't help me either and it takes me ten minutes to manipulate your long body so that at least most of it is lying down. You weigh nothing, but your legs are long levers and I can't move them easily.

"Help me, Dad," I whisper to you, to what you once were, as tears of frustration prick the back of my eyes. "Come on."

You don't help me, though, and in the end I manage alone and you are covered again. I stand with my hands on my hips for a moment and watch you. Then I sponge your mouth a little. I'm wide awake now, so I pad downstairs and put the kettle on. By the time I get back upstairs with a cup of tea and a book, you are lolling half out of bed again. My heart breaks some more.

The third time you try to get up I know we can't do this on our own anymore. I shake Penny awake.

"Pen. I need your help. Dad keeps trying to get out of bed."

"What?" She is blurry and squinting in the light flooding in from the hallway.

"Just get up, Pen."

She shuffles after me, but when she sees you sitting up, this time at the end of your bed, her eyes widen and I know she's awake. "What's he doing?" she whispers, as if you aren't even there; as if you aren't even you.

"I don't know," I find myself whispering back. "This is the third time I've had to get him back into bed. He's not awake. Not properly, anyway. I don't think he knows he's doing it."

Your whole upper body is shaking now and one foot lifts itself from the ground and then puts itself down again, clumsily, as if you're tapping your feet to a bad jazz record. We get you to lie down, but we can't drag you back up the bed and your legs are left hanging over the bottom.

"I'll get Davey," Pen says and dashes down the stairs. I look at you and sigh but I know she's right. We're just too tired to manage this.

The room is too small for all of us and we are cramped together as I try to explain what's been happening. Davey nods. Simon sways. "He's been getting out of bed? What's he doing that for?" His words are slurred and as he speaks I can smell beer on him. Suddenly it's obvious that the boys walked all the way to the little shop earlier. No wonder they were laughing so much when they got back. I grit my teeth as he leans into me. I suspect there's more than just beer at work here and I snap.

"Just wait outside, Simon. Davey can do this. You're in the way."

He recoils so much it's almost a pantomime response. "In the way? In the fucking way? He's my dad, too . . . I have every right . . ." His arm is waving as much as yours now as he points angrily at me. "Maybe he's getting out of bed because he doesn't want to be here! Have you thought of that, you fucking freak!" His dark eyes rage at me.

Penny pulls him away. "Come on, Simon, not in here. Let's go and get a cup of tea."

I don't say anything as he lets Penny tug him out into the corridor. He's still muttering, and then he shouts, "Paul told me you didn't want me here. You don't trust me. He told me!"

I want to cry. I want to cry because Paul doesn't understand how sensitive the boys are. I don't believe he told Simon that—I really hope he didn't, but I know Paul well enough to know that he would have spread his guilt. He would have told Simon that I was worried about the house. That I was worried about *what he might do*. Now two of them hate me. *Freak*. I wonder if I'm losing it. I try not to care and turn to you. Davey has got you all straightened out and pulls your duvet up to your chin.

"His hands are so cold. Probably best to keep them covered."

"Thanks, Davey."

He smiles sheepishly. I know he hasn't been drinking. I can see it in his eyes. I sip my now-cold tea and make out Simon's unsteady voice, still full of ire and hurt. Davey goes down to join them.

Not for long though, because within half an hour you're at it again. I can feel my seams coming apart.

It's a dark night inside.

8

There is very little sleep had that night and at about five a.m. rain begins to lash the house. Hard, heavy drops beat the walls and windows, but the rhythm soothes you. You finally settle down into some kind of comatose rest and I manage a couple of hours of escape in the chair. Still, even the bricks feel unsettled. You've crossed a bridge in the night and the change is tangible in the stale air of the morning. You are closer to dead than alive now. Even the house and the gray sky outside know it.

I hear the steady chug of an engine outside as a tractor rolls by. The world keeps turning. I yawn and stretch, bones cracking as they straighten and then I sponge your dry mouth. It doesn't wake you. This sleep you're in is different. I wonder if you dream in there. I talk to you anyway. It can't hurt.

At about eleven, after a quiet breakfast of coffee and toast, Penny takes a subdued Simon to the train station. We pay for his fare home and tell him we'll call when things change. He is still angry, his ire no doubt fueled by self-pity and more cheap beer consumed in the night. He doesn't look at me as he leaves. Davey shrugs a little and goes back inside.

Watching them leave, I feel something, but I don't know what it is. It's not anger, at any rate. I don't think I've got room for that. Davey is tidying up and rummaging through old things in the study so I make a cup of tea and go back upstairs. I plan to run a bath but, when I pop my head around your door, your eyes are open.

You try to speak but the words don't make sense. They're dry and rasping and confused. I try not to cry. For a second I wish you'd just come back or leave completely. This in-between is no good for anyone. A mistake in nature's plan for us. Better to be hit by a bus or drop out of the sky than this interminable changing. This memory thief. I stroke the wisps of hair across the top of your head. When did they get to be so white? I don't remember. You were always dark when we were children. Dark hair, dark eyes and dark, swarthy skin. I sigh.

"Simon's gone home," I say softly. "He'll probably come back in a couple of days. Paul too."

Your eyes fix on me and I smile. Somewhere in the glistening yellow and faded colors I see the ghost of the dark man who used to live in your skin. Oh, you're still in there, all right. If only for a little while longer.

"I think he was finding it difficult. They both were."

There is the hint of a raised eyebrow on your sunken face. I like to think there is, at any rate. I drip a little pineapple juice into your mouth and then your eyes shut and you're off again. I go for my bath.

"Hey, Sis," Davey calls to me from the utility room. "What the hell is this?"

My hair is dripping down the back of my sweatshirt, but I feel better for the wash. I feel clean. Fresh. I shuffle through to the back of the kitchen in my slippers.

"What? What have you found?"

He's holding the object up, examining its almost-round yellow-painted edges. He puts it down on the side and it wobbles on its uneven base. I laugh out loud.

"God, I'd forgotten about that." I pick it up and giggle some more.

"Yeah, but what is it?"

"It's an ashtray. Dad made it." A snort of laughter escapes me. "At the hospice."

Davey stares at me. "He made an ashtray at the hospice?"

I look at the terrible piece of sculpture in my hand and then up at my brother. "Yeah. Rude, isn't it?"

A smile stretches from Davey's mouth to his eyes as he shakes his head. "Can I have it?"

I nod. "Sure. Of course you can." I can see why he'd want it. It sums you up, really.

He takes it from me and stares at it. "I didn't even know he'd been to the hospice." He turns the ashtray over in his hands as if it is precious treasure. I don't mind Davey having it. He is a good boy. He has a deep soul.

"He only went a couple of times," I say, staring at the ceramic.

"So did the woman from the hospice come today?" I ask when I get in from the library. It's freezing outside and my nose is numb in the heat of the kitchen.

"Hmmm," you say.

I pause by the kettle. You're leaning against the radiator.

"Did you ask her about the day center?"

Your nose crinkles slightly. "Yes."

"And?"

"Well, she made it sound all very perky." Your face isn't convinced. "They have art classes and music classes. And they come and collect you and drop you off. On Wednesdays, apparently."

I pour us both a mug of tea and hand you yours. I've put some cold water in it. Your insides can't take the heat anymore.

"Thanks, darling."

I raise an eyebrow at you. "Are you going to go?"

"I can't decide."

I recognize that stubborn face and I try not to smile. "Well, what else are you going to do all day? Sit in here and watch daytime TV?"

You raise an eyebrow right back at me. "I like daytime TV."

I sigh. "God, you're incorrigible, Dad." I look at my watch. It was late closing at the library tonight and it's nearly seven thirty. "Speaking of telly, *Eastenders* is on."

You groan. "Do you have to put a dying man through that rubbish?"

"Shut up," I say as I flounce down the corridor. "Or you'll be dying a whole lot sooner than you expect." I'm smiling, though. How we smile in all this, I don't know. But we do.

The first time you go you come back in a grump. They wouldn't let you smoke inside. I point out that perhaps that isn't the most unreasonable request. You mutter something about stable doors and bolted horses. I smile. I don't think they've met a lot of people like you. Maybe a few that are a bit like you on the inside, but none exactly like you.

"I mean, we're all bloody dying there." You are rolling a protest cigarette on the breakfast bar as you speak. "So what the hell is wrong with having a room where you can bloody smoke? It would be a bit bloody hypocritical to quit now, wouldn't it?"

I shrug and keep my smile inside. You are feistier this week. Different medication. The lift won't last, but it's still good to see you almost yourself.

The second time you go the effect of the new drug is wearing off and when I get back from work you are sitting in the kitchen, your head resting on your hands. You sit up and smile as I put the kettle on.

"Good day, darling?"

"Oh, you know. Same old. Books come in, books go out." I smile. "And you? How was the hospice?"

You shrug. "I don't think I'll go back again."

I pull milk out of the fridge. This isn't childlike stubborn defiance. I recognize the finality in your voice. *No more biscuits before bed. No, you can't go out dressed like that. Your mother isn't coming back.* I've heard that tone in thousands of your words over the years.

"How come? Did something happen?"

"Not really." I can hear how tired you are. "But I can't give them what they want. They want me to fulfill a need in them, not the other way round."

I sip my tea. There's never just a straightforward conversation with you. "What do you mean?"

"They want to make me feel better about dying. To make *me* feel better about dying gives *them* a purpose." You pause. "But I'm fine about dying. And they just can't accept that. It takes away their purpose." You sip your tea and flinch. "And I'm buggered if I'm going to waste what's left of my time pretending to be terrified just to fit into someone else's picture of how things should be. I'd rather watch reruns of *Dalziel and Pascoe* on UK Gold."

I shake my head. No, they won't have met anyone like you before. "How did they take it? Did they try to persuade you to change your mind?" I feel a little sorry for the staff at the hospice.

"Obviously." You raise an eyebrow. There is a glint in the eye underneath. "Until they saw what I made in ceramics this morning. Then they gave up. I don't think they wanted me infecting the rest of the inmates with my free-thinking attitude."

"And what exactly did you make today?"

You pull the ashtray from your pocket and put it on the breakfast bar. I stare at the misshapen blob, but I know you well enough to know what it is. I smile a little and chew my lip. You're grinning at me.

"Oh Dad, you are awful. A bloody ashtray."

"Uh-huh. And it's better than that. I made four. I left the other three in the TV room just in case anyone fancies starting a smoking rebellion."

I look at you and still can't tell if you're being serious. We burst into laughter together, snorting into our tea and then go to find an old detective show rerun to watch.

You take the ashtray with you.

I look at the ashtray in Davey's hand and the memory seems to be too far away, not only a month or six weeks in the past. The ashtray is a relic from a lost civilization. "Look after it, won't you?" Davey nods, and goes into the kitchen to zip it away safely in his carryall. The doorbell goes.

"I've brought this for you."

Behind Barbara a middle-aged man carries what looks like a folded wheelchair. "Upstairs with it, love," she tells him. "Just along the corridor."

She looks back at me and squeezes my arm. "I thought it might make things a bit easier."

Davey and I follow her upstairs where the man is unfolding the contraption. It isn't a chair at all. It's a commode. It is ugly and out of place and, just like at the cemetery, my empty thinking space is filled with images of concentration camps. I don't know why. As far as I know they didn't have commodes in Belsen. Maybe it's just the sheer loss of human dignity that overwhelms me. Is this what it comes to, then? All that life and music and madness leading up to a gray steel chair with a pan in the seat?

The chair glares back at me. I don't want to touch it. I think that if I do then I will somehow bring it to life. Maybe it is haunted by all the bitter dying souls that have used it. For a second I see tormented faces in the weave of the canvas and then I blink them away and curse my empty thinking space.

I tell Barbara about you getting out of bed. I don't need to explain too much because even now one of your arms keeps rising from the covers. She nods.

"That's the terminal agitations starting." She squeezes my arm. "They'll probably last a day or two and then he'll settle back down." I love the lilt in her voice. It flows over me like a balm, even when I don't want to understand her words. They exist separately in my head and neither is good. Terminal. Agitation.

"But what is he trying to do?" I look at her as if she has all the answers. She doesn't, of course.

"I don't think he's trying to do anything, love. I don't think he knows he's doing it. His body's just shutting down." She tucks your arm back under the cover. "I know it looks disturbing, but it's normal in this situation. It'll slowly happen less and less as he slips further away from us."

She is respectful, Barbara. She doesn't pretend to share our emotion, but she certainly understands it. That's what the night-shift nurses don't have. They don't have her *care*. It is a special thing, that care. I hope someone in her life appreciates it.

"Shall I arrange for a Macmillan nurse to sit with him tonight?" She looks right inside me. "You look like you need a decent night's sleep."

I nod. That would be good. That would be very good.

When she's gone I clean out your mouth and talk to you. I think you're listening. Your eyes watch me as I moisturize your mouth. Your teeth are too big in your cheeks and I work the damp cotton bud gently around them, cleaning out the scum and saliva residue that's collected there. It doesn't bother me. Not like the jar used to. I guess we all adjust to things and the horrendous becomes normal.

Your arms still tremble and rise and I try to handle them like Barbara would but I don't think my grip is that subtle. My own body aches from the activity of the night and I think maybe I bruise your wrists a little as I put your thin limbs back under the duvet from which they are determined to escape.

"Sorry, Daddy," I whisper. "I'm sorry, Daddy."

Eventually, I perch on the bed next to you so that I can stroke your head and rest mine on the wall behind us. The plaster is cool and feels good and I let my eyes shut. They sting a little.

I don't know how long Penny has been gone but it feels like hours. It probably is. I wonder if Simon is on the train yet. I wonder if I'm ever going to see him again. I wonder what he and Penny said about me in the car. For a second I try to remember what I said to Paul in that white rage, but I can't bring the words back. I wonder if they're even important. I doubt Penny remembers them. She just remembers the *way* I said them. I think about the way she looked at me and I wonder if maybe I'm showing through my cracks.

When I realize I'm whispering aloud, I open my eyes. My hand is squeezed tight around your thin hair and you're looking up at me. You're definitely seeing me. I let go immediately, shocked by myself.

"Oh God, Dad, I'm sorry. I was drifting a bit. I'm sorry." I stroke your hair back into place and kiss the top of your head.

Your mouth is working hard trying to speak. "What is it, Dad? Do you want a drink?"

A slight shake. More in the eyes than the head.

"The toilet? Do you need the loo?" A nod.

"Hang on, I'll just get Davey to help." I kiss your head. It's hot. You're sweating. "Are you sure you don't want a wash, Dad? I can do it. I won't get the nurses."

I see hesitation in your eyes. You do want one. I can see. I think about that lost dignity you must be feeling and I want to tell you it doesn't matter. Not in the great scheme of things. This is just *the end*. It isn't *the everything* of you. And it's the everything we'll remember when the memory of this fades. I remember me and Penny in the bath splashing bubbles, you smiling behind the camera. Or maybe I just remember the yellowy seventies photograph, but either way those things are the everything. All moments that have arrived here.

I can't explain this, though. The words are tangled on my tongue and I'm not sure they would make a difference. Because I guess for you the everything is done and there is only the now. And in the now your loss of dignity is everything.

So instead of talking I go and get Davey to help me get you up.

We get you sitting on the side of the bed, the morphine driver hanging from your arm.

"He wants the toilet and a wash," I say to Davey.

"Well, he's not using that thing." His voice is indignant.

I know what my little brother is talking about without even looking out into the corridor. Maybe he can hear the ghosts in the commode too. I nod.

"I'll run a bath and if he sits on the loo then I can sponge him down. Can you help me get him in there?"

Davey looks at me. "You start the bath running, but I'll wash him. You change his bed sheets. Make it nice and fresh."

I am surprised. "Are you sure? I can do it . . ."

Davey smiles at you. "This is blokes' stuff, isn't it, Dad? Now come on, let's get you in the bathroom."

Davey is gently firm with you in the way Barbara is and I watch with awe as he half carries you, pushing the bathroom door shut behind you both. I watch the glass there for a minute or two and listen to the tone of Davey's voice as he talks to you. He talks as if this is the most normal thing in the world. Davey has surprised me again. He fights so many demons, but in the here-and-now he's got what it takes.

I'm crying as I change the stained sheets and I don't know who for. Maybe for all of us. Maybe just for me. There is a worm in my head that whispers that it isn't only Paul who doesn't think other people feel and think and care. And maybe the worm is right.

When Davey comes out of the bathroom and we've got you back into bed, I hug him. I hug him tight and I hope he knows what I mean by it.

Penny comes back with the baby monitor. When she proudly pulls the large box out of the Argos bag, I stare at it. Davey does too. She looks at both of us.

"I was thinking about it in the car after I dropped Simon off. About the way he keeps getting out of bed. And so, *voilà!*"

We still don't get it and she sighs. "It's a video monitor for babies. You set the camera up in the bedroom and then plug the receiver into a TV somewhere else. I thought we could bring the portable down from your bedroom into the lounge. That way we can see when he's trying to get up."

I look at the machine and then at Penny. She shrugs. "I was just thinking how awful it would be if he fell out of bed and we didn't know for a while. I couldn't bear it."

I look at her plump lips and perfect face and wonder how I ended up with the empty thinking space. It isn't fair. I should have thought of the baby monitor. I should have. But then, unlike Penny, I guess I never got to actually have any babies.

"It's a good idea, Pen," I say, and I'm glad my envy of her can't be heard. "Good thinking."

She doesn't say anything, but she smiles a little and I know she's pleased. I look at Davey making more tea, and Penny unwrapping the box and I think that sometimes I don't know them at all.

It takes us about half an hour to get it set up and we put the monitor in the kitchen. I turn the grill on to make more bacon sandwiches. We are pleased with ourselves, as if the monitor will actually solve the problem. It doesn't though. Of course not—it's designed to display the problem, not solve it. Our self-satisfaction doesn't last.

One side of the bacon has barely started sizzling when Penny scrapes her stool back. "Oh, he's moving!"

The three of us gather round the screen. The image is projected in a strange green color, which makes it even more surreal. I feel as if we're spying on you. Your legs slip over the side of the bed.

"I'll go."

And that becomes the pattern of the day. You barely settle at all, and I find that I am transfixed by the portable TV.

In the afternoon we take it into the lounge so that we can watch a movie, but my eyes keep drifting away from the big screen to watch you on the small one. The pale green light makes me feel queasy, but I can't help but stare as your toes twitch and I know that any moment now you are going to start those strange jerky movements. I wonder where the energy comes from. Your organs must be eating themselves to stay alive by now. That's if the cancer hasn't got there first.

The three of us don't speak much. Penny tries, but gives up after a while. Even she can't make this easy. My thighs hurt from running up and down the stairs and my neck throbs with the start of a headache. The tension is unbearable.

We have takeaway Chinese for dinner, which we eat silently. We get up twice during the short meal to get you back into bed. As I bite into a spring roll I wish with a breaking heart that you'd just hurry up and die. I don't feel any guilt. I know wishes don't come true.

Night falls, another circle of the clock done. I like to see the empty blackness outside. It lets me believe for a while that the whole world is within these walls. That nothing else exists. I don't want you and us diminished by the million others looking out into the blackness, listening to the clock tick away the life of someone they love. Penny goes to bed at ten. She's been asleep on the sofa for an hour and Davey gently wakes her. I can see he's tired too, whereas I am wide awake in my exhaustion.

"You take my bed, Davey. I'll stay down here."

"No," he says. "Don't be stupid."

I shake my head. "I'll wait up for the nurse. I'm not tired anyway and I want to watch some telly for a while. Maybe read a book."

He looks at me. I shove him a little toward the stairs. "Go on. Do as you're told." I kiss him on the cheek and won't take no for an answer.

"Thanks, Sis. Just shout if you need me for something."

His tread is tired on the stairs and I know he'll be sleeping in minutes just like Penny. He didn't need to thank me. I didn't give up my room for him. I did it for me. I can't bear to be away from that green screen. I'm not sure I can take the hard much longer. Things inside me, inside my head, are beginning to snap and I don't want to think about them.

The nurse comes at eleven. She is a strange creature, this Macmillan nurse. Everything about her is a whisper, as if she only comes alive in the night and even then not in a way any ordinary human would. Her cheekbones are high and fine and a wisp of dark hair has flown free from her bun. She is young, younger than me. Her feet barely make a sound as she glides up the stairs. I explain to her where the tea and coffee is and that I'm sleeping in the lounge and then I tell her about your agitations. She smiles serenely as if she has it all under control and then she settles into the chair in the hallway and opens her book. I don't see what it is she's reading, but it's a thick text and the writing is small. I watch her for a second before going back downstairs. I think maybe she is the angel of death in disguise.

I don't sleep much, but pull the duvet up round my neck on the sofa and watch you on the screen. I've got one of those ideas in my head. I think she's going to creep into your room, settle you down and then put a pillow over your face. I don't know why I think this. But it's in my head, burrowing away. I watch her go in to you several times as you try to get out of bed. She settles you. She doesn't put the pillow over your face.

At some point in the night I hear her make a cup of tea. You are keeping her busy I think, up there. I see you sitting on the edge of the bed and your eyes shine white in the camera's green night vision. I don't see you in them, though. They are strange and confused. And a little afraid. And then I see her ease you back down.

She leaves at six and I unwind myself from the sofa to say goodbye. In the dawn light I see the circles under her young eyes and the sympathy in them. She is pretty and delicate, but she is just human after all.

"I'll be back at the same time tonight. If you need anything in the meantime, just call the nurses. I'm sure Barbara will call in at some point." She smiles a little. "He should be calmer now, I think. His breathing is becoming more irregular, which is normally a sign that the agitations will ease."

I find it hard to understand her language. I just want to know what it all means. I think she sees this in my face. Her voice is soft. I wonder if it will melt into something like Barbara's as she ages. I think it might.

"Your father is moving into the next stage. His breathing will slow. The pauses between each breath will get longer and longer. It's called Cheyne–Stoking. He's not there yet, but I think in the next day or so."

She doesn't need to point out the rest. The rest I understand. *Chain-smoking causes Cheyne–Stoking.* The little rhyme forms a rhythm in my empty thinking space. The rhythm is like hooves on tarmac.

"Is he in any pain?" I ask.

She shakes her head. "No. The morphine and sedative are taking care of that. I've just changed them—upped his dose a little. He's somewhere between sleep and unconsciousness. Quite peaceful." She pauses. "I don't expect that he'll come out of it much, if at all, anymore."

She knows the weight of those words. You've gone where I can't reach you and you can't reach me. Somewhere in-between.

I thank her and let her out. The house suddenly feels cold. I turn the heating up.

9

I touch the walls as I creep upstairs to your room. Even as I trace the familiar light pattern of the paper it feels wrong under my fingertips. Things are changing again. And like all the most important changes, this one will be irreversible too.

The sky is lifting outside as day leaves the dregs of night behind and I feel as if I am the only person alive in the world, trapped in this moment, torn between the two states of existence. This is something tea won't cure.

As I pass my room I hear Davey snoring. It's a thick sound and if I'd heard it anywhere else in the world and had to pick the person that sound belonged to I would say

Davey without missing a beat. Maybe we are most true to ourselves when we are asleep. Or when the rest of the world is asleep. My heart pounds quickly in my chest and I don't know why. No sound comes from Penny's room. Maybe if I listened harder I could hear her soft, steady, easy breath, but I don't. Her breath will go on and on. I hope she doesn't wake up just yet.

The nurse has pulled your door to and it creaks a little as I open it. The sound doesn't disturb you. There are different doors creaking open for you, ones that I can't see and ones that you can't quite get to yet, but somewhere in that strange sleep I think you're seeking them out. I wonder how far down you've gone and whether the nurse is right and that you're gone for good. I like to think you'll find your way back to the surface just one more time. I think I need that one more time.

I sit by the curtained window, but I don't look out over the road and the field. There will be nothing out there. Nothing for me. There is no hot tingle in my bones. I watch you in the bed for a long time. Maybe an hour. Maybe more. You try to get out of bed once in that time, but the attempt is more half-hearted than the previous ones. Either you're sinking or the sedative she's given you is a strong one. Or a combination of both. I ease you down on to your back and you comply. The daylight that crawls into the room allows no softness. Your skin is yellow and your pajamas look ludicrous on you. My head flashes with images of the commode and the crematorium and that awful smell and then from nowhere I see you laughing at a barbecue at Penny's, a cigarette in hand, laughing because I've burned the tuna steaks and she looks fit to explode. Your teeth fit your face then. Your skin is tanned and firm. Your eyes sparkle.

I pull the cover over you and sit back in the chair, my face burning. Time unwinds, bubbles of time bursting, exploding in my head. Tension buzzes under my skin. I'm at breaking point. Or maybe just beyond it. Who knows? Inside I feel the distant drumming of hooves. I squeeze your fingers.

When I'm calmer I go downstairs. Penny is in the kitchen. She looks at me funny. "You okay, darling? I popped my head into Dad's room and you were just sitting there, staring into space."

I shrug. I can't think of what to say because I have no recollection of her coming in. I wonder at that. "Sorry, I was lost in my own world. Thinking about things. You know, Dad. The past. Stuff. Probably half asleep."

Hey, Lady Penelope. Nudge your sister, she's off again.

Penny hands me a cup of tea. "As long as you're okay."

I wish she wouldn't look at me like that. I grin and kiss her on the cheek. "I'm fine. As fine as can be expected, anyway."

She picks up her phone and pushes the call button. Nothing happens and she hangs up.

"I'm trying to get hold of Paul, but it's on answerphone."
She tries again to no avail. I snort and raise an eyebrow.

"Don't," she says, lighting a cigarette. "Things are bad
enough as it is. I hate that we're all upset and angry and
falling out. I hate it. And now we can't get hold of Paul."

She uses "we" because she thinks it makes her words less
accusatory, but it just makes them vaguely patronizing. She
hasn't actually fallen out with anyone. I don't think she ever
has. It's always easier to get along. I watch her try the phone
again and sip my tea.

"I know you hate that, Pen, and I'm sorry about what
I said to him." *Whatever the hell it was*, I think inside. The
place where those words should be is still blank. Just angry
white noise. I take a cigarette from her packet and light it.
"But he's the one who's turned his phone off. Not you."
I wave my arm around dramatically. "In the middle of all
this, he's turned his phone off."

"He can't deal with it, that's all," she says.

"That may be true," I answer. "But it doesn't make him
any less of a shit."

She doesn't say anything after that. I can see her trying,
those ridiculous swollen lips twitching, but even Penny,
who's always been so tight with Paul, can't really defend
him now.

She goes into the lounge with her cup of tea and takes
her phone. She doesn't say much more to me, but I hear her
ringing home and talking to little James. She probably tries

Paul again but I don't hear her talk to him and it doesn't surprise me. He's gone into hiding. Not as far hidden as you, but still out of our reach.

Davey gets up not long after and makes himself some toast. We don't say much. He goes into the lounge and I hear normality blare from the TV. A bulb flickers above me, threatening to go out. The house is subdued, just as we are. I wonder if the bricks feel anything other than the cold.

Eventually I go into the lounge and join the other two.

On the monitor, you are lying still in bed. Not even your hands are trembling.

"He hasn't moved since we got up. Maybe he's settling down."

I nod. "The nurse said it would pass."

There is silence for a while and I wonder if it's my imagination, but it feels as if the tension isn't just inside me. I can feel it between we three, tight as a tripwire. There is another snap inside my head. I need those breaks to stop. I need some peace.

"You know, I was thinking," I say, "why don't you go home for a day or so? See James. You could take Davey. Nothing's going to change here by tomorrow and now that he's calmed down and the night nurse is booked, it seems silly all of us just sitting here." I wonder if I'm rambling. All I know is that I don't want them here. They don't belong here. Not now. I look up to catch a glance go between them and I see all I need to see to know; they don't want to be here either. It surprises me. It hurts me.

"I was thinking the same thing," Penny says, "but I don't want to leave you alone. Will you be okay?"

I grin through tight, thin, unplumped lips. "I've been okay for the past few months, Pen. I can manage a night on my own."

She looks at Davey as if to say, *I can't do anything right*. She doesn't say that, though. She says, "Well, if you're sure. I'll have my mobile on. Call if you need me or there's any change. I'll be straight back in the morning." I nod.

They sip their tea and pretend they're not in a hurry to get out, but I see through their cracks. Just like I think they're starting to see through mine.

An hour later and we've hugged our goodbyes and made promises to call every couple of hours. As we hug I feel the solidity crumble. Watching the small, flash car heading away down the drive, it's crystal clear that we've fallen apart. We've fallen apart and we didn't even have the good manners to wait until you'd gone before we did it. I can still smell Penny's perfume in the hall when I shut the door and it forms a ghost of her. Everything is ghostly. Or maybe I'm the ghost and they're all real.

I wish my head wouldn't hurt so much. Or my heart.

The day goes by in a drift. I feel as if I'm standing still and the world is passing by, not touching me but avoiding me, as if I'm outside of its natural ebb and flow. Or maybe it wants me outside. I stand in the kitchen for a long time, staring out of the window at the ivy on the garden wall. I wonder how long the vine took to smother the bricks while I wasn't paying attention. When my feet get pins and needles I come round a little and notice I've made myself a cup of tea. It's covered with a film and stone cold. I think about making another, but don't. I open the fridge and think about food, but my stomach churns. I look at the cheese and bacon in there and think for a minute that if I stare hard enough I can see it slowly rotting despite the chill. I turn the thermostat inside the fridge up to four, but then I leave the door open. Let's see what the cheese makes of that.

Barbara comes round and I smile and let her voice caress me. It coats me and hardens on my skin. Then Penny calls to say that they have got back safely and to check on us. I hear my words, *Yes, we're fine, no change, love you too,* and they seem normal enough, but I'm glad when she's gone and I can have the peace back again. I'm waiting for night to fall. The daylight, gray as it is, makes me feel unsettled. I smoke a cigarette and stare out at it. I don't open the window, but let the acrid smoke fill the kitchen. Gray outside, gray inside. I go upstairs. The walls stare at me, accusing. I ignore them. They're not real.

The chair creaks when I lean forward and talk to you.

I talk for a long time. I tell you all this and more, but I don't think you hear me, even though I think I see you hiding in there, a little way down. It's hard to tell because your eyes aren't closing properly anymore and they're becoming coated in a milky film. Kind of like dogs get when they have cataracts. I look at your eyes with their marble sheen. Even your surfaces are shutting you off from us.

I talk anyway. I let it all come out. Everything. I want you to know everything about me because I can't know everything about you. I pour myself into what's left of you, hoping you can wrap it all up and take it with you. I talk until my throat is raw and dry.

When I'm done I sit in silence and watch you descend into your cells and beyond. I listen to the endless ticking of the clock. I listen to your Cheyne–Stoking. I think about the language. I think about the Macmillan nurse coming later and I think about Penny and Davey and Simon and Paul. My heart pounds a little.

As darkness falls my head thickens and I feel how alone we are here, you and me and the nightfall. The nurse will be here soon and that privacy will crack. I wonder about the monitor downstairs projecting your image into an empty room. I look at the Listerine and tears and anger spark in my eyes. I twist in the chair. My face is burning. I feel swallowed up by the emptiness and I want to be free of it. I've always wanted to be free of it.

It's black outside, in the nothing on the other side of the glass, but I squint and search out the black fields below. Scanning. Seeking. Hunting. I haven't looked out of this window for a long time. Not in this way. Not *really* looking. I wonder whether he will come tonight. It's been so long I sometimes wonder if I've ever seen him—*it*—at all. I wonder whether it was just brief bouts of madness. God knows the wildness of lunacy runs in our blood and no one would be surprised if we all turned out to be fey in one way or another. So maybe the occasional brief bout of madness is all my special gift ever was.

But still I look. Forty next birthday and looking out of the window for something that I haven't seen in fifteen years, if ever I saw it at all.

But it's one of those nights, isn't it, Dad? A special, terrible night. A full night. And that's always when it comes.

If it comes at all.

I push my face into the glass.

I stare so long my eyes hurt and nothing exists outside the frame of the window. I can feel veins throbbing in my brain, or so it seems. My head is too full of memories and I can't get them in any sort of order and they randomly attack me. You, me, him, all of us, even Mum. You all fill me too full. You've taken my empty thinking space. I pinch myself and wish for a drift, but it won't come. I rock forward, keening, trying to cry it all out. Trying to cry you out. Trying to cry away this waiting for you to rot into death. My throat tightens. The world glitters in the corners and my own breath threatens to choke me.

Sound throbs loudly and painfully and I squeeze my eyes shut for a second. The pulse spreads through my body from my skull to my toes and when I open my eyes I see the Listerine in the spit jar shaking slightly in the rhythm. I stare at it, unsure. Reality wants to twist away from me, but I grip it. The glass is shaking. I am shaking. The world is shaking. I feel the magic in the empty air.

I am alive with tension. I think my face might burn me up from the inside. The house watches you with me. You lie still and grab at a mouthful of slow air.

I turn back to the window and, panting like a small girl, I glance out into the dark and all I can see are red eyes and a whirl of energy. I smile. I knew what I would see before I looked. Something that was snapped inside heals as I watch. The creature dances in the road and in my soul. I see you and me and my lost babies in the clattering of those heavy hooves, in the dark hide that shines with sweat. I stare, and feel my heart sing.

The beast must feel it too, because it stops and whinnies, the base of the sound making me flinch, and it paws at the ground, sending shards of tarmac up to the sky like black stars.

It shakes that terrible mane and I know.

My nose is streaming with snot and I lick it and the tears away as I push myself out of the chair. My legs shake under me and my whole body trembles. I feel vaguely sick—sick and hot—burning-up hot. I lean over you and look into your milky eyes. I need to know. I need to be sure. The beast roars for me outside and as I sob I think—I'm sure—I see the tiniest red pinprick shimmer beneath the smell and the wasting and the nothingness that breathes reluctantly from where you used to live.

I smile. You understand. You know.

Very gently, despite the heat and energy raging at me from outside, I kiss your head. I leave my love there forever and my lips there for a moment, savoring your heat. One hand slips under and holds your skull gently as the other pulls out the pillow before laying you back down again. I watch you. Your breathing doesn't change. One exhale. Four seconds of silence.

I think of him. I think of the ivy. I think of the poor Macmillan nurse and what she will say, and then, my vision blurred, I say goodbye to your face and push the pillow down over it. I hope it doesn't hurt.

Your hands tremble slightly and then your back arches, and then nothing. It didn't take so very much for you to die, after all.

I step away.

I leave the pillow where it lies.

After a second I turn and run. I can't be late. I can't be late this time, not this last time, this last chance. I pound down the stairs, my legs heavy and solid. My feet slip on the kitchen floor, but I stay upright. I can hear sobs in my chest but they don't slow me down as I tear out of the back door and down the path to the gate. I don't look at the swings.

The night air is cold and my lungs burn as I suck it in, deep down inside, no Cheyne–Stoking for me, my legs desperate to reach it before it disappears. It always disappears. But not this time, please not this time. I turn into the road, my limbs aching and clothes sticking to me. My hair is slick to my face.

I have nothing to fear. The creature is waiting for me. It's always been waiting for me. I stand before it and wail as it roars and rears up, shaking the ground beneath us as it lands and then I grab for it, my hands entwined in that rough mane and I pull myself up, burying my face in its hot, sweaty neck. It smells exactly as I imagined it would. As it turns to the field, I am ten and twenty-five and forty next birthday, I am everything I will ever be and ever was. And I am alive.

The blackness of the field and the night stretch out before us as the beast and I leap the fence. I laugh and my hair blows out behind me as we gallop. I feel my hooves pounding through the night as I rage onward. Behind me, the lights from the house fade.

I don't look back.

ACKNOWLEDGMENTS

A big thank you to all at Jo Fletcher Books for giving this little book, which means so much to me, an outing in the big wide world. Also thanks to Neil Gaiman for much laughter and insight and, of course, my agent Veronique. You're all wonderful.